A ROANOKE STORY

Also by Deahn Berrini

Milkweed: A Novel
How to Earn Your Keep

DEAHN BERRINI

A ROANOKE STORY

Somerset Hall Press
Boston, Massachusetts

© Copyright 2017 by Deahn Berrini
Published by Somerset Hall Press
416 Commonwealth Avenue, Suite 612
Boston, Massachusetts 02215
somersethallpress.com

ISBN 978-1-935244-18-9 (1-935244-18-3)

Cover: Mishoonash by the riverside at Plimoth
Plantation's Wampanoag Homesite, made by Native
artisans by hollowing out a tree by fire. Photo by Deahn
Berrini courtesy of Plimoth Plantation.

Drawings and map by Charlotte Leblang.

Library of Congress Cataloging-in-Publication Data

Names: Berrini, Deahn, author.
Title: A Roanoke story / Deahn Berrini.
Description: Boston, Massachusetts : Somerset Hall Press, [2017]
Identifiers: LCCN 2017037344 (print) | LCCN 2017041113 (ebook) | ISBN
9781935244196 | ISBN 9781935244189 (softcover)
Subjects: LCSH: Indians of North America--First contact with
Europeans--Fiction. | Roanoke Island (N.C.)--History--16th
century--Fiction. | Roanoke Colony--Fiction. | GSAFD: Historical
fiction.
Classification: LCC PS3602.E76358 (ebook) | LCC PS3602.E76358
R63 2017
(print) | DDC 813/.6--dc23

LC record available at https://lccn.loc.gov/2017037344

Preface

What we commonly call "The Mystery of the Roanoke Colony" has all the elements of an enduring myth of the settling of the United States: adventurous settlers, the first European baby (Virginia Dare) born on American soil, unknown and potentially hostile Native Peoples, and, then, the colony's wholesale disappearance, along with the unsettling truth that we really don't know what happened to 115 English men, women, and children.

The agreed on facts are these: in the summer of 1587, under Queen Elizabeth I of England and by the "charge and direction" of Sir Walter Raleigh, 115 English settlers were deposited on the eastern shores of what is now called the United States of America, in North Carolina. Shortly thereafter, England went to war with Spain and it took two years before a ship could be sent to check on the nascent colony. When the supply ship arrived, the colony had disappeared.

What is less known is that the English had made two previous exploratory trips to this same location. The first, in 1584, consisted of two ships that stayed for a few weeks. The second, arriving in April of the following year, 1585, consisted of seven ships and six hundred men. This second group included a renowned scientist, an artist, and soldiers. The ships returned home, and left 117 men behind to fend for themselves. The following spring, in 1586, the 117 men were picked up and returned to England, under murky circumstances that included an early hurricane and a destroyed resupply ship.

This group of 117, led by Ralph Lane, set the stage for what was to follow. These were the first Europeans that the Roanoke, the Native Peoples of that region, encountered. The Europeans on any ship that followed would have been viewed through the lens of that initial encounter.

Lane and his soldiers were veterans of a brutal war against Ireland. Lane's account of their sojourn on Roanoke Island speaks to the English inability to understand the Native People that they encountered. Their response to their unlikely situation was a military one, based on force and domination.

Any attempt to solve the "Mystery of the Roanoke Colony," then, must begin two years before, when the first English set foot on the shore. This book tells the story of the people whose fate was most changed by this initial encounter: the Roanoke.

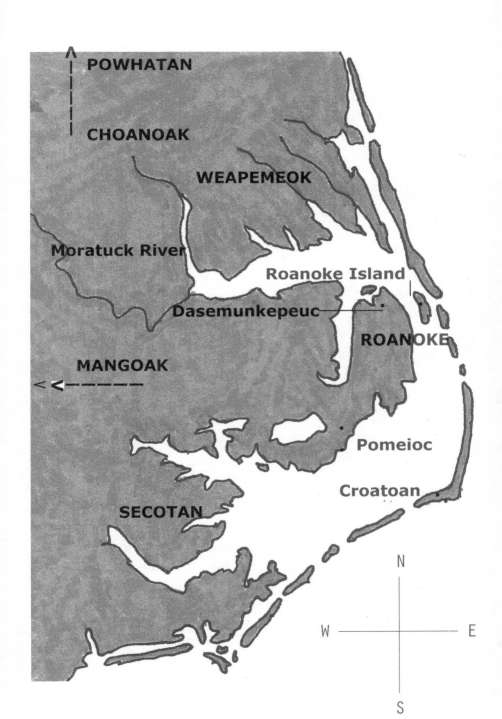

Summary of Characters

The names and terms in this story may be difficult for some English speakers. They are taken from modern Native People words, historical diaries, or from the *The Natick Bible*, also known as the *The Eliot Indian Bible*, which is the *Geneva Bible* translated from English to an Algonquian language, in 1663. Please take your time to immerse yourself in the different sounds.

The Roanoke Tribe:

In Dasemunkepeuc (a settlement on the mainland):

Adchaen (hunter of deer): Warrior, father of Keeta, husband of Mama/Nunnootam.

Asku (he who watches or waits): Warrior, friend of Menuhkeu.

Auwepu (a calm): Friend of Keeta, older sister of Naanantum.

Chepeck: Healer and spirit guide who cares for the sick and the dead.

Chogen (blackbird): Boy who gathers plants.

Ensenore: Older warrior.

First Mother or **Nootimis** (oak tree): First Wife of Wingina, charged with many responsibilities.

Keeta or **Adtoekit** (she who comes next): Daughter of Adchaen, warrior of Roanoke, and Mama/Nunnootam.

Kehchis (he who is superior by age): Older warrior, now in charge of dressing animals.

Mama or **Nunnootam** (she who hears): Mother of
Keeta, wife of Adchaen.
Menuhkeu (he who is strong): Warrior, son of
Wampeikuc, husband of Keeta.
Mese (little canoe): Young, unmarked boy.
Minneash (berry): Keeta's sister-in-law, married to Owush.
Mishontoowau or **Mishoo** (boy who makes himself
heard): Keeta and Menuhkeu's son.
Moskeke (toad): Man who plays the prey in hunting games.
Naana (she takes care): Younger sister of Auwepu.
Namohs (fish): A family of fish driers.
Owush (hawk): Warrior, Menuhkeu's older brother.
Pishpesh or **Pishpeshawau** (he blossoms): Son of
Owushaog and Minneash.
Pog (running water): Warrior, friend of Menuhkeu.
Rikopqua (inker): Woman who performs inkings.
Wampeikuc (osprey): Warrior, father of Menuhkeu.
Wanchese: Warrior, spirit traveler.
Wautog (she who knows): Plant woman and midwife.
Wequassus (swan, bright creature): Keeta's mother in law.
Wingina: Weroance of Roanoke.
Wunne Wadsh (beautiful nest): Wife of Wanchese.

On Roanoke Island:

Aquandut (bluefish): Warrior from a family of shell
polishers.
Granganimeo: Weroance of Roanoke Island,
Wingina's cousin.
Hashap (spider's web): Warrior, Aquandut's brother,
maker of traps.
Kautantowit (southwest wind): Wife of Granganimeo.

Nippe (still water): Youngest of the captured Weapemeok.

On Croatoan Island:

Manteo: Warrior, spirit traveler.

Other Tribes:

Choanoak: Ally to the north, to whom the Roanoke
    bring tribute.
Menatonon: Weroance of Choanoak.

Mangoak: Fierce enemies to the west.

Secotan: Ally to the south-west.
Pomeioc: Secotan village.
Peimacum: Weroance of Pomeioc.

Powhatan: Fierce enemies to the north.

Weapemeok: Ally to the north.
Aquascognok: Weapemeok village.
Okisko: Weroance of Weapemeok.

English:

Barlowe: Weroance on the first ship.
Harriot: Spirit traveler.
White: One with white leaves.
Grenville: Head weroance of the wassadors.
Lane: Thick-fingered weroance who cannot sit still.

Glossary

Appowac: Tobacco.
Bi-Bo: The north wind.
Kichi-Odgig: The great fisher weasel.
Kizi: Month.
Memegwasi: Spirits in fast-moving waters that tip canoes and cause drowning.
Nanabohzo: Giant hare who helps humans, from the time of the origin of the world, the good brother.
Mishibijiw: Water panther.
Pagwadjinini: Forest spirits.
Wapeih: Soothing plant.
Wassador: People of metal.
Weroance: Leader, chief.

A Blanket of Rabbit Skins

Prologue

"Tell me your story," the young girl asks. Her round face glows, reflecting the fire's restless flickers. Rain lashes at the roof mats.

"You have heard it all before," the old woman answers softly. She gathers her scattered memories, the thoughts like acorns rolling from a fallen basket.

The families lay quietly about the skins. They listen to the gift of water, enjoying the moment of rest. "Yes, yes, we have heard it all before," laughs the young mother. "That's why we ask for it again."

The woman shifts against the rabbit skin, sits up straight. She is older now than most of her people, but her recollection of things past is clear.

There is a brief stillness in the wild noise of the storm, and into that void she throws her voice.

"My story is the story of my people," she begins. "For I am everything and I am nothing."

The Roanoke

The Roanoke people lived along the river-sea, at the place
where the water shifts from sweet to salty, and the land from
clay to sand.

Through time, they settled into three villages—Croatoan
Island, Roanoke Island, and the largest, Dasemunkepeuc,
which sat on the mainland and housed the chief.

To the north and west of these villages lay larger tribes.
These greater tribes, counting more warriors, occupying
more land, and with a firm grip on the inland trade routes,
allied with their smaller coastal neighbors and let them be.

The larger tribes wanted and received three things from the
Roanoke: their prized polished shells, their bountiful dried
fish, and their position as a buffer between the safe inland
and the mysterious sea. For the eastern coast was a tenuous
and changeable marshland, and the open water beyond a
vast and potentially dangerous gateway.

What lay over this broad expanse of water? More water?
Was it the land of the dead? Or a land populated with
dangerous and powerful creatures? Only the Creator knew.

Thus far, what dangers had the waters brought? At the
mouth of the bay lurked hungry Mishibijiw, the water panther. Storms rolled in on the waves from the northeast and
the south, carried by violent winds that drove giant floods
far inland.

This only, until stories of strange sightings of large canoes
came to be traded up and down the coast. Objects appeared
in the sand, made of an unknown metal, harder than the

familiar copper. Occasionally a body washed in with the tide, pale and clothed in strange skins.

Uneasy over these changes, the inland tribes stirred. The Roanoke, rich in shells and fish, would not be moved. They were the buffer, and a buffer understands that if the familiar rests on the one side, the strange will always push on the other.

Dasemunkepeuc
Keeta Learns a Lesson

Keeta raced through the grove of ancestor trees, her bare feet flying over a soft bed of needles. The blue jay urged her on with a cackle, "Run, Keeta! Run faster!" Patches of light flashed on her face, and she closed her eyes each time the sun caught her to enjoy the red pulse behind her eyelids. Halfway through the cedar stand, she met the ocean's cool breeze. When she reached the grasses, the wind was full on her. She stopped and scanned the sands.

The boys ran along the beach like busy terns as they collected sharp shells for arrowheads and scrapers, and looked for rocks to anchor the fishing weirs.

Menuhkeu, taller than the others, drew her attention. A sloshing gourd of water in hand, he snuck behind Asku and doused his head. Keeta laughed with Menuhkeu. Asku shouted in surprise. Spinning quickly, Asku reached out and narrowly missed catching his friend. He set out after him, but Menuhkeu's long legs kept him several lengths ahead. Menuhkeu laughed as he ran, slowing only once the game was his to let Asku catch him and retain honor. They wrestled briefly, circling and nipping like fox kits in the sand.

Enjoying the joke, Keeta pushed away the thought of where she, as a girl, was supposed to be—the inland field, weeding. In a burst she had run away from this task, and she wasn't going back now, not while the wind felt so cool and the boys were so amusing. Keeta crossed the beach to the shallows to let the incoming waves roll gently against her legs.

Once cooled, she joined the boys in the search for shells.

Although Keeta had seen only eight summers and had never been taught this skill by an elder, she had watched many arrows crafted in her father's house and was confident of the qualities of a useful shell. The boys were shy at first of her, whom they knew well but not in this role, working like a boy instead of a girl.

She dug a strong whelk from the wet sand and placed it in the communal basket. "That's a good one," commented Asku. He smiled. The praise emboldened her and she skipped over the beach like a sandpiper in the fall, bending down to scoop treasure, running up and down with the waves on the wet sand.

The summer afternoon lengthened.

How long First Mother stood at the edge of the grasses watching, Keeta couldn't say. A piercing twinge at her shoulder made the girl turn her gaze to the ancestor trees. Shadows hid most of First Mother's body, but the sun hit her legs, and Keeta recognized the intricate pattern of First Mother's inkings—her calves bore the marks of a net, like a weir. An indication of her high status, these linked diamonds widened gracefully up to her thighs.

And that net pulled Keeta in, a little fish caught. The boys stopped their work and stood straight and silent as Keeta retreated to First Mother across the sands. Keeta didn't look up at Menuhkeu's face as she passed him, but she felt his sympathetic eyes on her.

When Keeta reached the grasses, she followed several paces behind First Mother to show respect and to acknowledge that she had left the fields without permission, before the work was finished.

What had made Keeta leave her work so suddenly? The girl thought back. Inland, the sun had shone hot and steady, and she remembered stooping among the tall plants without rest, her pile of pulled weeds increasing faster than those of the other girls. The air had been so still, Keeta heard the rustle of a small snake making its way through the corn, and the cicadas cried and were silent and then cried again.

A shadow passed over Keeta as she followed First Mother deep into the ancestor trees, trees older than memory, trees protected like the corn was protected, the ground cleared beneath them. The broad canopy shielded Keeta and First Mother from the sun and its heat. Strands of light moved and danced along the broad trunks of the darkened grove. As quiet as the forest first appeared, it wasn't still. To walk among these trees was to feel the spirit of the people whispering in the moving branches.

First Mother sat at the base of a trunk and gestured that Keeta sit across from her, against a neighboring tree.

She lowered herself onto the ground. The dead leaves soft against the back of her legs, the bark firm against her back, Keeta breathed in the sweet-musty cedar, a pungent odor she enjoyed. First Mother threw a handful of appowac in a semicircle, closed her eyes while she offered her thanks, and inhaled deeply. Keeta waited, upset that she had caused First Mother to come to the beach, uncertain of what would happen next. She closed her eyes as well, but each time the girl tried to calm her thoughts, the insistent complaints from a squirrel up above interrupted. His fast chatter echoed her too-fast beating heart. The jay, the troublemaker who had earlier happily urged her to run, to run as fast as she could, was silent.

When she opened her eyes, First Mother was watching.

Keeta stopped her fingers from pulling at the blue flowers sewn onto her skirt. "I am a girl, First Mother, and my legs are bare," she said. "I forgot your wise words."

First Mother watched her so intently that Keeta wanted to look down at her clasped hands, but Keeta knew that she must not hide. She thought of her Mama and wished she were sitting with her under the tree.

If First Mother were a black bear, proud and fierce, a guardian, Keeta's Mama would be an egret, rare in her beauty, and sociable.

Keeta's Mama was the one whose body breathed closest to hers when they slept, the one whose arms held Keeta tight in the wet winter winds, the one who combed walnut oil through her hair, and the one who wove blue flowers on her deerskin skirt. Keeta was her only daughter, her only child. The brothers and sisters who had come before and after were not granted passage to this world, but made their way directly to the Creator. Keeta would meet them when she returned to the world of the dead, her Mama told her, and she would share the stories of all they had missed of their life here. So Keeta kept track and paid attention, so that she would have something to tell when her time came.

"Keeta," said First Mother. Keeta was grateful she didn't call her Keeta-stand-too-straight, as some of the older girls did. "Just as the Creator guided our ancestors, we must let ourselves be guided by those with greater knowledge. Some boys may want to plant corn and some girls may wish to sharpen shells into arrow points. Yet, what if at one moon-of-setting-corn no girls wanted to plant? We would starve come winter. What if no boys found shells for arrows? When the Mangoak came in from the west, we would have no defense. What would a girl with a warrior's arrows do when her time has come to bear children? The Creator will measure our actions when we pass from this world by how well we have served our people."

"Yes, First Mother," Keeta answered, but her words were tiny.

First Mother nodded and rose. "Sit here until your ancestors come," she said. "Then return to the village."

Keeta sat a very long time against the hard bark of the

ancestor tree while the sun lowered. Her breath returned in steady pumps. Her shoulders loosened, and she felt a twinge of hunger and some weariness.

She sat up straighter. Boys when they reach twelve summers must leave for a full phase of the moon and fend for themselves away from the village, so Keeta understood that this was a far smaller test. Still, she worried for Mama, who must be wondering what had led her daughter down to the water.

Gradually, the pick-pick-picks of the woodpecker and the random rustling of life moving through twigs slowed. The shadows softened, and the grove grew dim. Soon she would smell the bustle of the skunk, hear the hoot of the owl. Keeta leaned harder into the bark and turned her palms up to the sky. She breathed deeply to gather the cedar scent and firm her heart, and just in time, for her ancestors began to crowd around. There were so many! They prodded sticks into Keeta's legs to see what she was made of, sniffed at her oiled hair, and fingered the flowers on her blue skirt. She was uneasy at their familiarity, at what they would do next, but she didn't open her eyes or run away. They made her remember the hot afternoon of weeding and the two girls a few rows over, Naana and her older sister Auwepu, working side by side.

Always together those two! thought Keeta—Naana in her lazy way reaching her hand under the root and turning her wrist so slowly, managing only half the pace of her sister Auwepu, who chatted to her softly. Keeta felt a burning unhappiness in her throat. Together all day, and asleep at night on the same skin, those sisters, always talking and not to her! Keeta remembered digging hard into the ground with her stick and watching as Naana sat back on her heels to stare at the ospreys circling slowly above for prey. Then Auwepu's laughter wafted toward her like rustling corn leaves in the breeze, and Keeta's heart had felt even sadder. What could be so funny? Could they be laughing at her? That was when she wanted to join the boys. This idea had hooked into her like a claw, and she had leapt up and run. Next, the ancestors showed her Auwepu and Naana's surprised faces, full of worry as she left the field so suddenly. Keeta saw then that her actions weren't hers alone.

Then a small turtle appeared, with a shell in diamonds of browns and blacks. Keeta felt the hard turtle covering on her own back and the stretch of her skin as the shell broadened and grew, the patterns widening with the shell. Would she become a turtle too? Was turtle trying to teach her?

Dusk gloomed. The blinking sparks of fireflies lit up at her feet, and her heart felt full and strong. Auwepu and Naana were with her. First Mother guided her. Mama waited for her to come home. Never alone, Keeta understood, we are never alone and our ancestors guide us always.

Through the half-light of the evening, Keeta quickly found her way home. She left the chatterings of the forest creatures and headed toward the chatterings of her people as they sat around their fires, visiting in the long, warm evening.

She entered the fire circle and her Mama's arms found her, her warm body pulling her in. "I'm hungry," said Keeta, and her Mama laughed and moved to get her some stew and Keeta followed, unwilling to let her go too far.

First Mother stood up, a smile on her broad face. "Sit," she said kindly. "I'll get the child some stew." How long had she sat visiting by the fire, waiting for Keeta's return?

Her father, Adchaen, rose from his seat, and came to her and kissed the top of Keeta's head as she sat close to Mama.

"Thank you," said Keeta when First Mother handed her the stew.

They sat as she ate the warm ground corn and summer berries, a favorite. When she was done, she watched the red of the low fire. Tired, she felt close to sleep. Thinking of the fireflies, of the feeling that had come to her, Keeta understood that she should share what the ancestors had shown before she forgot.

"I saw... I was..." Keeta willed her thoughts to words. "I was a small turtle, but I grew large. My shell pulled at my back." She reached her arm around to feel her back, and the touch of her soft skin reassured the child that she hadn't changed. "The shell had many shapes of blacks and browns and..." She could no longer see the shell, so she thought carefully about how it made her feel. "It was heavy."

The adults listened. In the low light, Keeta watched the shadows move across the webs on First Mother's legs and the side of her father's face, nodding as she spoke. Mama leaned gently into her. Was that Wanchese standing just outside the fire, his long crow feather visible in profile? Why was the spirit traveler listening to her, a girl, and her story of turtles? She shifted closer into her mother's arms.

"You are my girl, like none other," her father said, pulling Keeta's attention back to the fire circle. First Mother laughed softly.

That night, when they lay down on their mats to sleep, Mama held Keeta's head against her chest and stroked her hair. Yet, despite her gentle touch, the girl could not erase the heavy feeling of the weight of the turtle shell on her back.

Dasemunkepeuc
Menuhkeu Hears a Warning

As the sun fell behind him, Menuhkeu, grown to fifteen and now a warrior, gazed east to the broad, glassy bay, tinted orange in the lengthening rays. Beyond, between the barrier islands, the sea tossed. Rumors of large canoes coming from beyond the horizon and landing to the south were rife at the last green corn festival, a gathering renowned for its news and gossip. Did the young warrior hope to see one? He wasn't sure.

His father whistled and Menuhkeu trotted back to where Wampeikuc knelt on the hard, wet sand of low tide. In one easy motion, the older warrior lay his bow down by his side and flipped an arrow from his quiver onto his broad palm. He pointed to the head, a whelk shell sharpened to draw blood on touch, and to the tail, sanded ash ballasted by the tight feathers of a blue jay. "See how the feathers are of a similar size? How they sit evenly around the shaft?" He tapped his finger at the tip. "See how steady it sits? How sharp its point?"

Menuhkeu nodded, even though he had heard this particular lesson so many times that his father's words often filled his head while he was making his own arrows, as he had for several seasons now. His father's voice, steady, sure of its rightness, had also guided the council from the time Wampeikuc had become a warrior.

"Before the arrows go into your quiver," Wampeikuc concluded, "you must inspect each one to make sure it's true. A weak arrow won't find its target."

Menuhkeu possessed the strength and the will to follow the same warrior path as his father, but he didn't share his father's fondness for speech. Only room for one big voice in a lodge, the older men joked, but out of Wampeikuc's earshot they questioned the taciturn boy's reluctance to speak his mind.

The fading light turned peach, and still father and son waited on the shore, away from the reeds that surrounded the nearby fresh-water pond, for the wind to come and cover their scent. With his right hand Wampeikuc pinched a portion of appowac from the leather pouch that hung at his belt. He threw it in the direction from which he wanted the wind to come, the northwest, and asked the winds to stir so that the hunt could begin.

An osprey, Wampeikuc's spirit bird, appeared above a cloud tinged gold. Air lapped at Menuhkeu's back. A high-pitched whistle from the hunters waiting closer to the reeds alerted the pair to pick up their bows.

The hunt began. Menuhkeu and Wampeikuc ran soundlessly across the sand toward the patch of thick rushes.

When they reached the reeds the two moved apart. They halted on the beach side of the marsh, downwind of the fresh water. The slight rustling as their fellow hunters took their places mimicked dry reeds clacking in a breeze. Forming a living net of bowmen around the pond, they crouched and watched across the water to the woods on the far side. Soon it would be dark, but the time just before the night fell was a good time to take deer.

A shadow and a quick movement and a small doe appeared at the waterside. The arrows held, and what was expected followed, two smaller babies. In a few more months, as the days darkened and the young ones fattened, they would all be taken, but not now. Menuhkeu's fingers tingled in anticipation.

A large buck appeared, visible only in movement, so

close was the brown of his coat to the hue of the darkening brush. Wampeikuc let go the first arrow and a hail followed. Menuhkeu let go his first arrow, and just before he let go the others, he spied a second buck, just behind the first, its antlers a glimpse of motion. He readjusted and aimed at the second deer. Pierced three times in rapid succession, it fell quickly. At the low call, the men and boys brought their bows down and sprinted to the fallen bodies before the scavengers arrived.

Menuhkeu's buck gave off the strong scent of blood leaving. His side heaved weakly in a dark pool. Menuhkeu took a fifth arrow and shot the animal's neck, for a slow death is reserved for enemies. He bent over the animal as life left and thanked him for his offering to ease the creature's leaving. Although he had uttered these words of thanks many times, in the presence of such a sacrifice they never failed to ease him as well. Then he twisted the arrows out from the wounds.

Pog, a warrior in the same age group as Menuhkeu, followed just behind. He took in the buck and Menuhkeu's handful of bloody arrows, all with their familiar blue jay shafts. "Look," he shouted loudly, "he took it on his own! What a selfish trick!"

Menuhkeu filled at once with embarrassment and pride. "Pog! Others had arrows in!" he protested, moving slowly away from the buck.

Thin and wiry, Pog turned the carcass over and grabbed its legs to tie together for easier transport. Asku, who had just arrived with a carrying pole, set the pole down just behind Menuhkeu's ankles as Menuhkeu stepped backwards, sending him tumbling down into the wet marsh.

His friends howled with laughter.

Surprised and wet, Menuhkeu lay sprawled on his back and smiled. He held the arrows up toward the sky. "Creator," he said, "we thank you for your blessings, for strength comes to us as a people, and one warrior's arrow is a stick in the wind."

Asku slipped the pole between the deer's tied ankles, Pog took the other end, and the group carried the meat back to camp. Not once did Menuhkeu claim the prize as his own.

His older brother, Owush, watched the scene from a distance with a small smile. At the same age he would have been unable to resist claiming the victory, for Owush knew he had too much of his father in him.

The old warrior Kehchis scurried out of the temporary hunting camp to greet the plenty. Before the night was over, he and the boys would prepare the bucks to hang. Then, they would skin them and separate out the different parts, each for a specific use and each handled its own way, as the ancestors taught.

The hunting party of early fall included almost every warrior from their village, from those whose markings were long scarred on their shoulder blades to those whose markings were still raised and red. The easy weather allowed any warrior who could still run and see sharply to participate, even Old-man-with-a-sharp-tool-Kehchis, who was not always called Old-man-with-a-sharp-tool Kehchis. He was once a fierce hunter and warrior, one who had taken many deer and even a few cougars.

As dark came on, several torches were lit around the camp.

Menuhkeu claimed a gourd, ladled in a portion of stew, and joined the others around the fire. The soup was rich with just-ripened squash and beans, chunks of venison, and dried berries. He breathed in the flavorful scent and felt the good—warm winds, no cold, plentiful and varied food, and all the warriors together in a successful hunt.

A young warrior squeezed in next to him. The image of four arrows that marked him as a warrior of Wingina, weroance of Roanoke, were fresh on his back, yet he was eager and familiar. He nudged Menuhkeu.

"We should go back to that pond every night," he said. "We could store enough meat to last until spring."

Menuhkeu laughed out loud.

"What's so funny, Menuh?" asked Asku.

"The boy's planning our hunting parties now."

"It was such a good spot," the young warrior insisted. His bony frame held a big spirit.

Pog gave him a punch. "You can't think clearly with a warm belly."

"You can't think clearly with an empty one, either!" the boy responded.

"Brother deer is not a fool," said Menuhkeu, after the laughter had quieted. "He won't return to a spot marked in blood."

The waning moon rose and a fellow hunter, the screech owl, announced his presence. Outside the perimeter of the fire many pairs of eyes glinted, drawn by the light—raccoons, fox, coyote, looking for scraps.

The stars peeped out as well. The food stored, the smaller torches were put out, and the men sat together around the large fire. Wampeikuc told the story of their hunt, how they had chosen their spot, how they approached the pond, and how the wind had blessed them. Menuhkeu heard how his father turned the story into a series of lessons for the younger boys and how some of the older warriors asked questions to which they already knew the answers. He laughed to think that, as a boy, he had wondered why the best warriors continued to hunt for details after the kill: the smell of the wind, the type of feather used on a shaft, the angle of the sun. Now he understood the purpose of going over and over the hunt—to pass down the lessons as well as to always remember them.

When the three-quarter moon was high in the sky, the fire was doused and the younger warriors lay down on the soft ground wrapped in light skin blankets.

Gradually the camp fell still, surrounded by quiet. Menuhkeu dropped easily to sleep. Sometime later he was awakened by the unsettling, rhythmic calling of a barred owl, two short bursts of hoots followed by a longer one that rose and fell. He wondered if he alone heard the warnings—again and again the call to the other hunting owls, stay away, stay away, stay away. He pictured the fluffed-up creature, with its sharp beak and talons, its overlarge eyes, a creature that swallowed his meal whole and excreted pellets of bones and teeth in tight bundles on the forest floor. So noisy and then so silent in flight, a deadly silence that allowed him to sneak up unannounced on his prey, those smaller creatures who were warned again and again of his coming, but still could not manage an escape.

Dasemunkepeuc
A Dark Cave, Blue Flowers, and Brother Herring Returns

The spring moon night had lent its chill to the morning,
so Keeta, Auwepu, and Naana wore thick winter moccasins on their brisk walk beneath leafless trees. Sunlit lichen,
a shimmering yellow green, spread on the north side of
the trunks. So many birds had returned that their singing
set the woods stirring, breaking the silence of winter.

The three carried their baskets to the storage cellar to
gather acorns for grinding. Over the cold months since
the last harvest, the corn had disappeared, berries became
a memory, and the remaining venison dried bits, barely
big enough to mix into a stew of the last mashed beans.

As the winter went on, each time the young women
visited the cellar they had to reach deeper and deeper into
the dank earth to fill their baskets. On this day Auwepu
disappeared into the storage cave once and then again,
and the time between returns stretched out as she searched
farther in. Keeta and Naana didn't speak of it. To occupy
her time, Naana found a handful of white trillium and
tucked it into her pocket for Wautog, the old grandmother
who had begun to teach her about the different powers
of the plants.

"What's that one for?" asked Keeta.

Naana just smiled.

Keeta nodded, it was a question she shouldn't have
asked. The plants had many uses, and it was best to let
those who knew keep track of these differences. She let the
warm sun fall on her face and wondered about the corn

festival this coming summer, when she would certainly be old enough to dance.

Auwepu emerged from the tunnel a third time. The baskets were nearly full, but her face looked pale and her lips were a strange color. Keeta laid her hand on Auwepu's arm, its surface little bumps. "You're cold," she said.

Auwepu shrugged, and Naana looked carefully at her sister.

Keeta, annoyed at herself that she had let Auwepu do the bulk of the work, hurried down the entranceway with the last empty basket before Auwepu could protest.

Loose dirt shifted against her moccasins at the sloped entrance. The winter air hit her as if she'd dived into water and all was black. Her body cried to turn around and return to the surface. She waited a few heartbeats until she could discern the shape of the cave and feel its emptiness. So quiet, so dark, so cold. Was this how it was in the world of the dead?

"Keeta!" Naana cried out into the opening. "What are you doing in there?"

Her voice startled Keeta. How long had she been caught in her thoughts? "Coming!" she replied as she took stock of how low the piles of acorns and chestnuts had become throughout the winter—still it would be enough to bring them into the next season. They had given the Creator their work all winter long, rebuilding nets, baskets, clothing, tools, and arrows by the fires, and the Creator had provided.

Back above ground the warmth welcomed Keeta like a friend as her eyes blinked to adjust.

The three were quiet as they set out on their return, their baskets heavy upon their shoulders. Keeta pushed away the dark mood of the cellar when it tried to follow her back to the village.

And there, in a sheltered patch favored by gentle winds and sun, she saw them, blue myrtle! Naana followed her glance and gave a cry, her basket tipping to the side. Auwepu stepped forward quickly and righted it before the tricky Pagwadjinini had a chance to make them spend their morning refilling spilled baskets.

Laughing like that, their baskets barely righted, they looked up and saw Menuhkeu standing just ahead of them on the path. He had stopped, watching, his bow down, a string of felled rabbits tied onto his belt. The light slanted across him and his dark hair glistened.

For the second time that morning, Keeta's body had feelings her mind raced to catch. She had known Menuhkeu through thirteen seasons, and now she couldn't speak. She felt poised at the lip of a high rock—spirit open to the falling, yet feet still on the ground.

"Menuhkeu," Auwepu teased. "I'll trade my basket of acorns for your rabbits."

He peered at Keeta so intently that she looked down at her winter moccasins, but he answered Auwepu in his usual easy, quiet manner and made a story about how running to catch the animals had tired him, making Auwepu, Naana, and Keeta laugh. Keeta wasn't sure if she'd imagined his look, so unaware the others seemed of it.

And then he was gone down the path.

They set out walking again.

"Keeta," Auwepu asked after they had walked almost the whole way back to the village. "When you are a wife, will you still wear blue myrtle flowers on your skirt?

By Naana's expression she could see that the sisters had discussed this between them.

Keeta's face burned. The delicate blue flowers her mother had lovingly sewn were no match for the wild beating of her heart. "No!" she blurted. "Only girls wear flowers on their skirts."

They walked in the silence her words had carved out. "Maybe your daughters will wear them," Naana said at last. "They're so pretty."

On the last turn to home, Mese, a young, unmarked boy, burst down the path. "I have news!" he cried out. "I have news! We were on the sands playing the fish game," he began in the tone of a child about to begin a long, wandering tale. Keeta and Auwepu exchanged impatient glances. They had heard more than they wanted about the fish game, a rough wrestling match in which some players link strong arms and become the net and others run loose and are the fish, and the favored conversation for all small boys.

"Mese," Keeta blurted. His excited face switched so quickly to concern and confusion that Keeta regretted at once her quick words. "Mese," she repeated in a softer tone, and his smile returned. "What is your news?"

"Our brothers have returned! Come down to the sands with your baskets!" he shouted and took off running again.

They hurried along and soon saw that Mese had delivered right words. The village resembled a hive of honeybees at the first swarm of spring, all in motion, finding baskets and nets, busy with the making of cooking fires and setting up posts for broiling.

Oh the joy! The joy at the return of the brothers, the herring and the sturgeon, to offer themselves to the people!

Nets were woven and ready, set-poles placed in the icy waters of the bay, they had waited for a third of a moon. During the time of waiting, the people worried. Had they set the poles too soon? Would Bi-Bo and his angry north winds reappear and pull them all out? The Roanoke had offered appowac so that their brothers would return again and the people were patient, but hungry. And now they were here!

Auwepu, Naana, and Keeta stored their acorns under mats in the lodges and raced to the shore with empty baskets to join the others.

On the beach the wild spring winds sent clouds running across the broad sky, but the sun was steady. What pleasure those many glints flashing in the water, like a mica river running in the sea.

The people had spread out snakelike in a line along the shore and into the bay. At the head were the stronger men in their canoes, taking what they could with their spears. In the shallower waters, men and women waded into the cold to transfer the fish trapped in the weirs into the baskets. The laden baskets were then passed along to those on the sand, and brought back to the village.

Keeta found First Mother, a look of glee on her normally quiet face. "Here, take this!" the older woman commanded and handed over a basket of the slithery fish, still jumping with their last breaths. Around them were excited voices, full of anticipation for the feast they would have.

And this is the gift of the Creator. The fish stay until the sun is high enough for the first planting, until the berries return and the bear comes out of her cave. Thus, during the empty time when there is little left to eat, the fish brothers offer themselves to the people.

All that evening Keeta sat around the fire with the rest of the village and feasted on broiled fish, with its crispy skin and delicate, flavorful flesh. The weroance, Wingina, gave appowac blessings, as did the spirit traveler, Wanchese. Even the children stayed awake until the stars were bright and many in the sky.

Mama told the story of Kichi-Odgig, the great fisher

weasel. Keeta watched Mese, tired from running in circles for most of the day ferrying messages, his eyes closed and resting against his mama, sit up straighter when the story began. All the children loved the story of Kichi-Odgig.

It begins like this, in a time of no summer, like the time just passed.

The time of no summer had lingered because a jealous and selfish hunter had captured all the summer birds, keeping them bound inside his lodge. Kichi-Odgig, the fisher weasel, that clever and hungry creature, had had enough of the winter weather. He decided to release the birds so that summer could return. Kichi-Odgig waited until the hunter was away and snuck into his house. Once inside, herring, who was visiting the hunter, wanted to cry out in alarm, but the fisher weasel covered herring's mouth in pitch and then bit through the ropes to release the birds. Just as the last of the birds shook their cramped wings and flew to freedom, the herring's mouth broke its bond. He shouted to the hunter, "Your birds are fleeing!" The hunter, who loved the birds, came running at once with his long spear and, in great anger, chased the fisher weasel.

This is the part the children loved best and they looked upward in anticipation. In his escape, the fisher weasel climbed higher and higher until he was into the sky but not before the hunter threw his long spear at the fisher weasel's tail.

At this point, Keeta's Mama threw open her arms and called out in a large voice: there he still is! And all looked up at the great fisher weasel, Kichi-Odgig, lounging on his back in the sky, his tail hanging limp behind him. Unlike some of the other stars that come and go with the kizis, the fisher weasel is always in the sky for all to remember. And so, thanks to Kichi-Odgig, each season returns to the people, and the herring repays his debt by arriving just before the summer so that there will always be enough to eat.

This is the story of the people, of their many blessings, and their great joy.

Dasemunkepeuc and the Barrier Island
Swim Like a Bird, Fly Like a Fish

The high-summer afternoon sun lit the coast. The water glinted, and even the shade held warm, moist air. Brother herring had returned to the sea, and the second planting of beans, corn, and squash ripened under the powerful sun.

Out of the berry-rich woods came the call, "pee-a-wee, pee-a-wee." Passed from scout to scout, "pee-a-wee, pee-a-wee," the message travelled rapidly until it reached the outskirts of the village—a friendly visitor approached.

Shortly a messenger from Croatoan arrived along the path, his body wet with sweat. He slowed as he reached the packed earth of the clearing. Four arrows inked on his right shoulder marked him as Wingina's warrior, and his broad face was familiar to many, as Croatoan was the neighboring village perched on an island south, down coast.

He had news, he said, for the weroance Wingina and for the village.

Wingina quickly called a council. The messenger's news would run like a fire through fall reeds, and he thought it best to gather the people together to hear it. Wingina strode on his long, spindly legs that resembled those of a crane toward the meeting ground, some shorter-legged advisors jogging slightly behind.

The Roanoke arranged themselves into the circle. Once the fire was alive, Wingina lit the appowac and passed the hot pipe around—to Wanchese, the spirit traveler with his crow feather in his hair; to Wampeikuc, Wingina's trusted advisor; to First Mother; to Ensenore the elder, whose skin had tightened around his muscles, leaving him looking a little like a bulging sack of squash; and to Chepeck, the keeper of the dead in his rabbit cloak. The pipe then went to all the respected warriors and elders who had gathered, as well as to the messenger from Croatoan.

As a young warrior, Menuhkeu sat just outside the fire circle. One day, perhaps soon, he would pull on the long pipe of appowac and gather guidance from the Creator on behalf of his people. The village gathered and spread out around him as the afternoon rays slanted—young boys whose quick motions conveyed their eagerness for adventure, skeptical adults who had lived with rumors of visitors from the sea all their lives. Keeta came with her Mama, quietly sitting so they could hear the talk in the center. How else to know when one's voice would be demanded?

Menuhkeu watched the messenger when it came time for him to speak. The Croatoan opened his mouth, but no words came out. He shut it and waited. He spread his wide palms on his thighs.

A seagull shrieked above.

Keeta looked up at the bird as it headed toward the beach.

Menuhkeu wondered why the words stuck inside the Croatoan warrior, a person he recognized as full of talk on the playing fields.

"Huge canoes are coming," the messenger said at last "Blown by the wind, yet always heading north."

A slight rustling indicated people heard, but no one spoke.

Whose canoes? thought Menuhkeu.

"They move like a bird on water or a fish in the air," the messenger continued.

Ensenore, as the eldest, spoke into the quiet as those seated tried to picture what the messenger had described. "Wanchese should be the one to greet these visitors," he suggested. "They may be from the spirit world."

"Or they could be attacking from the south," countered Wampeikuc.

Keeta wondered how these two advisors could speak of plans, so stuck she was on the image of a bird behaving like a fish and a fish like a bird. She tried to clear her head and listen more carefully.

The talk went on in this vein, with some thinking the spirit world had sent messengers and others convinced the southern tribes were coming to expand their shellfish ground, until Wingina spoke. All voices quieted at the weroance's voice. He asked the runner, "Have you seen these big canoes?" In the pause that followed he added, "With your own eyes?"

The messenger shook his head. No, he had not.

Wingina let this information sink into his audience.

Keeta felt relief, while Menuhkeu felt let down, a loosening of his limbs. "We will send out scouts," Wingina offered, as heads nodded all around him. "These scouts will travel down the coast."

At this, Menuhkeu kept his eyes straight ahead, not daring to look to his right, at Asku, nor to his left, at Pog. They each wanted the honor. They each wanted the excitement of hunting something they knew nothing about.

After the council, only Pog was left disappointed; Wingina chose Menuhkeu and Asku to investigate the Croatoan rumors.

The two young warriors paddled for the southern island that separated the bay from the wilder sea, a long stretch of sand and cedars and pines entirely within Wingina's alliance. Once they landed, they headed south, they set no fires and carried only corn meal to mix with water and whatever greens they came across.

Within those dense woods, thick detritus blanketed the sand, leaving a soft, soundless path. Trees offered shade from the sharp summer sunlight. By the third day the warriors reached the end of their territory. At the far end of the island, they stopped.

The morning found them resting against the trunk of a cedar tree, their eyes trained on the moving sea. Menuhkeu chewed on a strand of beach grass. The bitter taste kept him awake in the lull of the waves pulling in over the shore. Asku fingered an arrow, his thumb moving lightly over the tight circles of string that tied the feathers to the shaft.

In the growing heat, the morning sun found its way through the trees, shifting around them in soft patches of light. Menuhkeu's thoughts went to Keeta, to the upcoming green corn festival, when she would be old enough to dance.

Asku nudged him and stood. "Wake up."

Menuhkeu shook his head of his wandering thoughts and nodded up at Asku. "Let's continue down the beach."

But Asku was not looking at his friend. Menuhkeu followed his gaze. Asku pointed.

Menuhkeu stood. Barely visible to the south, a dark speck floated briefly on the water before it disappeared. It came and went on the horizon like this until it remained in sight, and then it grew bigger. After a while a second dark speck appeared and disappeared and then remained, like the first.

The young men stood hidden in the trees and watched.

Asku breathed deeply. "They do move with the wind."

The two canoes sat high on the water and soon grew large, each as large as a village. Menuhkeu squinted at the vessels and saw no oars, only large sticks pointing upward, with large mats of white. Like the runner had said after his long pause, these canoes moved in the wind, like a bird on water or a fish in the air. Menuhkeu marveled he had described it so well, so strange was the sight. He felt the strangeness enter his body and run through his limbs with his blood. The two friends, accustomed to a lifetime of banter, said nothing as they watched.

The sun travelled across the sky. The shapes approached and took form.

The Roanoke didn't take their canoes so far out on the open ocean. There was no need to, for everything they needed was inland or in the river or the shallows near the beaches.

Asku broke the long silence. "It's time to bring the news back."

Menuhkeu considered Wingina's question to the messenger: have you seen this with your own eyes? They could now answer yes. Between the northern barrier island close to Dasemunkepeuc and the southern one on which they stood was a gap. In that gap lived Mishibijiw, the water panther. There the currents shifted and ran with great force—even if these large canoes could fit through, they might have a hard time making their way to the protection of the bay. Yet, this was the only entrance between the sea and the bay for a long distance.

Menuhkeu had been taught since birth that the one constant of life is its motion—the sea moving backwards and forwards, the rivers flowing toward the rising sun, the moon making its way westward across the sky, and children growing up into adults who die and pass on to the next world. Within this continuous motion, the rhythms didn't vary—corn, squash, and melons came in the warm weather, acorns in the fall, fat deer in the winter, and herring in the spring.

This looming canoe, though, came from an unfamiliar place, a world best interpreted by a spirit traveler, not a young warrior. "Yes, my friend," he answered Asku. "Let's go."

Dasemunkepeuc and Roanoke Island
The Visitors Are Made of Metal

Two days later, the large visitor canoes appeared at the place where Mishibijiw lived, where the sea flows into the bay. Many in the village gathered along the beach, hidden among the ancestor trees, to watch.

On the soft ground beneath the cedars, Keeta sat next to Auwepu and Naana in the shade, their arms linked. They, along with the other girls and women, had spent the last few days picking all that was ripe and near ripe from the fields and hiding it away, as if for winter. Then, tired of secondhand stories, they had come to see the huge vessels for themselves.

Big as a village, the canoes sat high on the water, carrying tall posts like limbless trees and large white mats that flapped when the wind gusted. "Will the water panther attack them?" wondered Auwepu, half in dread and half in hope.

Keeta scanned the rough surf in the distance, the foam white with anger. "Maybe," she answered, worried more about who was steering the canoes, for it seemed they had turned toward the bay with purpose, with no fear of Mishibijiw. The canoes tilted as the white mats shifted. One after the other, the vessels came through the passage between the islands, rolling far from side to side in the surf.

Keeta's breath grew shallow. She picked at the flowers on her skirt. Naana pressed closer in.

The canoes settled in the bay. The white mats collapsed and what looked like weighted ropes fell out over the side. Shortly, a sharp noise boomed. A sensation like thunder hit Keeta's chest and ears. At the force of it, several children cried and ran away toward the village, and a flock of nearby cranes scattered into startled flight. The birds shrieked and called as they reassembled themselves in the air and fled down the coast, chased by a thick and foul smoke. This smoke hung briefly above the canoes before the wind took it out to sea.

The stark image of the departing cranes wasn't lost on Wingina, nor his cousin, Granganimeo, the weroance of Roanoke Island. Both cousins were members of the crane clan, tribal leaders who managed relations with outsiders.

Granganimeo, a large man with a convivial manner, worked to make sense of the strange canoes. He reminded those hidden with him in the cedars at Dasemunkepeuc that the Creator manifested all beings, and so their best option was to take the part of the host. "It's better to invite them into our land. That way they will know that this is ours, that they are visitors." This despite the precarious position of his own people on Roanoke Island across the bay—closest to the large canoes, they had prepared to leave their island for the safer shore of Dasemunkepeuc on short notice. What had kept them put were the midsummer crops of corn, beans, and melons, nearly ready to harvest.

"If they're the stronger warriors, we must show the right respect," pointed out Ensenore, in awe of the strangest sight he had witnessed in his many seasons.

"They must prove themselves our betters first," answered Wampeikuc, who also worried at their display of strength and power.

First Mother listened, glad that, unlike on the chillier Roanoke Island, the majority of the second planting of Dasemunkepeuc lay hidden, secure in winter storage, and glad as well that every household in the village was ready to flee inland.

Menuhkeu too heard danger in his father's words. He wondered at how one is to be brave when faced with mystery.

His friend Pog broke the silence. "They have no manners! The large canoe belched like a thunder god and left a stink afterwards!"

Wingina turned his head in Pog's direction. Pog, deferent apology on his lips, held his tongue when his weroance laughed loudly. Indeed, Wingina appeared relieved. Perhaps he was most worried that fear might settle in and cloud his people's thinking.

The canoes sat. In the villages of Dasemunkepeuc and Roanoke Island, corn still had to be ground, traps mended, and fields attended to. No one appeared on the shore in sight of the visitors, and Wingina and Granganimeo set a strict watch. After two days, as the sun reached the middle of the sky, a smaller canoe was dropped down over the edge of one of the larger ones and lowered into the water. Several figures clambered down ropes on the side of the larger canoe and into the smaller one. With a small white mat attached to a single pole, the small canoe moved forward toward the sand beach at Roanoke Island.

The Roanoke warriors guarding the shore watched as the figures sitting in the strange vessel came into clearer view. There were eight of them, two in the front, three on one side, two on the other and one in the back. The sky was white and the air damp. Gradually the dull sheen of figures appeared, and then mouths, chins with hair, noses, and eyes came into view—they were men. Their clothing strange, the outer layer reflected light like copper, or mica in a rock, as if they were made of metal, of wassador.

The small canoe tipped steeply up and down as it rode the shallows. At their approach, one figure stood and pulled down the white mat. The scouts hidden in the trees heard the visitors' shouts, but they could make no sense of their words.

With awkward splashing and thick legs they stepped out

of their canoes. Each held a carved stick, and they wore large, shiny hats on their heads. Four walked forward onto the sand, sticks pointed outwards. The others dragged the canoe up to the beach.

A small group, they stood uncertainly on the sand. They looked warily around. The Roanoke warriors saw then that these visitors didn't know what they would find on the beach, and that this not knowing frightened them. The visitors walked for a small distance on the sand and made one brief foray into the cedar woods, staying always together in a group. After a short while and much discussion among them, none of it understandable, the visitors returned to their small canoe and made their way back to the large canoes.

In the discussion afterward, Granganimeo counseled again that the strange ones be greeted as guests. "Look at their guarded faces, their bodies tight and alert, their short walk onto the sand, their avoidance of the trees," he said. "It points to their obvious unease, if not fear." Thus the Roanoke decided to greet the visitors in a formal manner, as if they were greeting a visiting tribe. The preparations began the following day.

In the filmy light of early morning, Menuhkeu left his lodge with his brother Owush and their father. They made their way toward the stream closest to the village, where the water still ran and hadn't yet flattened out into the marshes.

Fog disguised the familiar path, and moisture hung in the air. It rested on the barks, on the leaves, and on the webs laced on the grasses. In the mist Menuhkeu heard the rustling motion of others walking along.

The growing light revealed thick fog rolling over the stream, wrapping the Roanoke warriors in a shifting, chilly cocoon. In the grayness Menuhkeu watched disembodied hands washing a leg and saw Owush's head floating alone in the white. He shook these images out of his mind, sure that such strangeness invited no good.

Dipping his gourd in the stream, Menuhkeu cleaned himself by pouring chilled water over his entire body, beginning with his head. His skin prickled in response and his blood woke up.

After they bathed, the warriors grouped together to apply their colors. Asku took the reed brush dipped in paint and formed the bold, broad stripes of yellow and red that indicated allegiance to Wingina. The colors gleamed in the fog. Menuhkeu dipped his brush in deliberately, to harness his strength. The paint was thick and, stroke by stroke, he daubed his chest, his arms, his legs, his face, and turning, let his friend complete his back.

The friends had performed this ritual for the first time just after their moon-long sojourn to become warriors, three seasons ago, and Menuhkeu felt its power grow with each repetition. When they were covered in the paint, they became one person—strong, courageous, dedicated to their people.

When the warriors were finished, Chepeck, who wore his rabbit cloak for the occasion, burnt the appowac by throwing it into a lapping flame. The pungent scent of the offering would ensure that no harm would befall the Roanoke when they accompanied Wanchese the spirit traveler in the first part of his journey to contact the visitors.

Wanchese wore no paint, only his black crow feather that indicated his vocation as spirit traveler—interpreter between what is learned from the body and what is learned from the spirit, between the ancestors and the living, between other creatures and humans, between the familiar and the strange. Although not tall, Wanchese was strong in the chest, a warrior, a father and much trusted. The Creator had chosen him to bridge the diverse worlds, and he offered himself willingly to each journey.

As the sun nudged its orange ball over the eastern horizon, the warriors left the shores of Dasemunkepeuc and paddled across the bay to Roanoke Island, with Wanchese at the rear. When landed, they pulled up their canoes, and ran as a group to the cedar trees. Menuhkeu stood hidden with the others as his father and the warrior Adchaen led Wanchese onto the sand. There they stood, waiting to greet the wassadors.

The fog dissipated and the day turned bright and blue.

Figures discernible only by the glint on their hats gathered along the broad walls that ran the length of the large canoes. Wanchese raised his hand in greeting. He strode up and down the beach to indicate his intention to meet peaceably. Wampeikuc and Adchaen held their bows.

After a time, a very small canoe appeared and was lowered into the water. This one had no white mats but was moved by paddles, two on a side, and held four visitors, again carrying their sticks. The canoe chopped through the water toward the beach.

Sticks held high, their canoe hit the sand. One jumped out and held the canoe in the water, and then the other three threw their legs over the side and into the water with a splash. Wanchese once again raised his hand to indicate a peaceful greeting. The visitors walked toward him, stopping within an arrow's reach but outside fighting distance. Their bodies hidden in their clothing, Menuhkeu stared at their faces, familiar, yet very hairy, with very light skin. Their tight expressions revealed unease, although their stances portrayed firm resolve.

Searching for the spirit traveler or weroance in the group of metal-clothed visitors, and finding none and having none offered, Wanchese welcomed all the visitors, wishing them well after their journey on the sea, far from their home. He told them that they were the guests of Wingina and the Roanoke, and that Wingina sent greetings.

The men didn't respond but stood staring at Wanchese and Wampeikuc and Adchaen with frequent glances into the woods behind, as if they sensed the presence of the warriors hidden within. Wanchese continued, telling them again that they were welcome and that no harm would come to them.

One of the guests, a squat man with yellow hair on his face, stepped forward. As he did so the others held tight onto their sticks, objects that to Menuhkeu were clearly weapons. The yellow-haired man spoke in response. His words were short, his speech brief. He took another step forward, bent his body over at his waist, raised himself back up again, and spoke some more. Through his gestures, it seemed he invited them to join him in their small canoe to make a trip to their large canoe.

Wanchese turned to Wampeikuc and Adchaen. "I will go now," he said. He followed the metal men into their square canoe and took a seat near the back. They paddled him back to their camp on the water.

The warriors waited for Wanchese's return, unsure of how long he would be gone and wondering at what point they would need to go after him. The sun rounded the sky, its rays lengthening to white.

For as long as Menuhkeu could remember, Wanchese had been Dasemunkepeuc's only spirit traveler. Roanoke Island had none. As a boy, just before Menuhkeu had traveled his moon-long quest away from the tribe to become a warrior, his father reminded him to look carefully for signs—from the ancestors, or Nanabohzo, or brothers from the plant or animal world, any indications of guidance. Menuhkeu had returned from his moon quest more assured and aware, but with the same intention with which he had left: to hunt with the same great skill as his father and older brother. His closest friends and deer clan brothers, Asku and Pog, had returned with the same goals of perfecting their traditional warrior skills, keeping to themselves any revealed guidance meant only for their learning.

Menuhkeu recalled one boy from Croatoan Island, however, who had returned full of talk. Menuhkeu hadn't paid close attention at the time, mostly because the Croatoan boy, the prized son of a weroance mother, had not been an easy companion. "Hey," Menuhkeu called out to his friends who waited with him for Wanchese's return, "do you remember the odd one from Croatoan Island? The boy who did his moon quest when we did?"

Pog, who had lain back to consider the blue sky between the tips of the pine branches, sat up. "The one who returned wearing the cougar skin?" He snorted.

"He spent most of his time tracking that cat," added Asku.

"But he returned saying he had been shown the way of the spirit traveler," answered Menuhkeu. He thought of Wanchese, still on the big canoe. Although he could not imagine what Wanchese was doing, the Creator had guided him there. The Creator had found him capable of mysteries Menuhkeu could not fathom.

"Wanchese might have had the same odd ways," said Asku, as if he could hear his friend's thoughts, "when he was younger. We don't know..." His thought trailed off. With the tip of his thumb, Asku tested the tension in the sinew of his bow. "We don't know what it requires, not having been asked to try."

Menuhkeu had watched his friend check and recheck his weapons for many years now. He understood the gesture. Unlike Wanchese, who had learned other skills, this was what they knew of bravery.

At long last the visitors paddled Wanchese back to Roanoke beach. When the metal ones had returned to their canoe,

Wampeikuc and Adchaen emerged from cover to receive Wanchese. He handed them a soft bundle. Before he retreated to fresh water to bathe, he spoke a few words to his old friends. "They are men," he said, and held out his hands palms up, to indicate the simplicity of this conclusion. "And, like men, they have come to see what they can get. They say they have come to trade."

Adchaen nodded and Wampeikuc smiled. This they understood.

The Visitor's Canoe
*Granganimeo and the People of Roanoke Island Accept the
Invitation to Visit With the Strangers on Their Big Canoe, and
Trade*

Menuhkeu paddled his own canoe alongside the visitors'
much larger one. In the soft breeze, wide waves flattened
harmlessly against the giant canoe's broad side with a steady
slosh. The larger vessel barely shifted.

Up close, Menuhkeu admired how the wood of the canoe
had been much worked on and fit together. Its sides rode
high on the water. Beneath the waterline, barnacles had made
their home on the long stretch of smooth wood. Menuhkeu
wondered when these creatures had latched on, how far they
had traveled to arrive in this bay.

His passengers, three aunts and four young cousins from
Roanoke Island who had chatted in anticipation as they
rode across the sound, turned silent when their small canoe
crossed into the shade cast by the larger vessel or "ship," the
strange word Wanchese had taught them that meant "very
big canoe that travels over the sea."

A young cousin threw out the rock to anchor their canoe.
Menuhkeu's passengers looked up at the web of ropes that
hung flat against the side of the ship and formed a path to
the top, and hesitated. Kautantowit, Granganimeo's garrulous wife, called down to them from the ship, "What are
you waiting for? You are the last to arrive!" The young cousin
reached out and grabbed a hold of the rope with both hands
and pulled himself out of the canoe. He turned back to his
fellow passengers, "It's fine," he assured them as his mother

handed him a large melon. Using his feet and one hand, he climbed quickly up the net. When he reached the top, he turned back with a wide smile, holding the melon over his head with glee. The aunts laughed. Shyly at first they held onto the rope and, distributing the melons amongst them, they climbed one-handed up the rope-path to the top of the ship, bantering with Kautantowit along the way to hide their nervousness.

Menuhkeu ascended last. The cool air that hovered over the water warmed as he rose. At the top, he looked down, and his own canoe looked very small.

Stepping over the wall and down onto the ship, the breeze died. A rich, not-pleasant smell greeted him. Kautantowit had moved with the aunts to investigate the ship, her thick row of copper armlets glinting in the sun.

Menuhkeu was charged with guarding the place of coming and going. Short of leaping out of the ship and a long way over into the water, it would be difficult for anyone to make a quick escape. He took note of Asku, Pog, and the warriors he knew from Roanoke Island, their bodies relaxed but their bows and hatchets within reach. Numerous strange wood and metal objects and the many Roanoke Island families, who had come out of curiosity and in hopes to trade, crowded into the small space, much like the home of a large clan in winter.

The shiny ones, the wassadors, had their own guards, the men who stood at intervals holding their weapon sticks, faces as unyielding as their metal clothing. Not wishing to alarm these people who were now his hosts, Menuhkeu stood still where he had entered, by the path down to the canoes. He watched white-skinned wassadors in soft clothing move about the ship. They climbed what had appeared to him as sticks from a distance, but were really massive poles, like tree trunks, covered in intricate weavings of rope and mats.

Menuhkeu wondered if his people could be taught to make their canoes move with greater speed as well, but then he considered how clumsily the strangers had approached the beach and how far over their ships had tilted when entering the bay. Were these large ships made only for the sea?

Menuhkeu kept track of his people moving over the ship, the aunts unwrapping bundles of melons, elders with polished shells, the pride of Roanoke Island, to trade, and the children, shyly reaching their fingers out to touch the unfamiliar surfaces.

The foul smell intensified. Flies buzzed insistently.

An aunt had handed a man in soft clothes a melon, now balanced on a wooden platform. From a pouch at his side, the wassador pulled something that flashed as he raised it high in the air and brought it down on the melon. The melon split neatly in half with the blow.

Menuhkeu reached for his bow as the Roanoke threw out cries of wonder at the tool. These were interspersed with the briefer, guttural sounds of the wassadors, who marveled at the fruit.

Emboldened by the excitement, a Roanoke boy climbed a second ladder that led toward the mats, his head arched back as he looked eagerly up at the web of ropes. Children peered into recesses of the broad wooden expanse. Some looked down at the water, tipped far over the edge, their feet wiggling off the floor, their heads out of sight.

The older man with the polished shells gestured emphatically with a white man in soft clothing, who stood back, shaking his head, holding his stick. Menuhkeu watched Asku move in their direction, his hand near the club in his belt.

"Brother," a young warrior from Roanoke Island asked, "have you seen the food?"

Menuhkeu shrugged, his eyes on Pog. "Nothing here smells like you'd want to eat it."

The warrior laughed. "Perhaps they're waiting until we're very hungry so we will enjoy it more."

Pog had joined Asku, near where the elder rolled his shells back into his skin pouch as if to store them away. Pog stared out over the water, his fingers curled slightly at his thigh. Menuhkeu wondered what his friend was up to.

A loud crack split the air, followed by a foul smell, a sound smaller but much like the thunder sent out when the two canoes first came through the gap into the bay.

Several children cried out and raced to find their mothers. The man with the shells jumped back. The wassador with the smoking stick narrowed his eyes, his mouth quivering in apparent satisfaction at his effect. Menuhkeu watched the smoke seep out of the stick and felt his blood race too quickly. He wondered at the stick's power, whether noise and smoke were its only dangers.

A wassador with yellow hair on his face, who Menuhkeu recognized as the one who had spoken on the beach, strode over, talking expansively. He took the stick, pointed it this way and that, as if to demonstrate its use. Granganimeo, who had responded to the explosion by coming toward it, stood in front of the shell man. The yellow man didn't hand the stick over to let the weroance examine it, just as a warrior never hands over his bow. Granganimeo nodded and smiled, but all the time his eyes followed how the yellow man handled the stick.

Gradually talk renewed, but the mood remained lowered after the use of the noisy weapon. Kautantowit called to her husband. "If there is to be no food," she announced clearly, "perhaps it is time to leave." Granganimeo gave the sign. The people began to leave the ship, small canoe by small canoe.

In the confusion of movement that followed, Pog strode by and slipped Menuhkeu a small bundle, which Menuhkeu transferred without question into his quiver.

The aunts were somber on the return trip. The one who had brought melons left with a copper bowl, which she turned this way and that, offering it around for examination.

How to explain why no food had been offered? Or appowac? How to explain the tiredness that hung in their limbs after the outing, when no work had been done?

Menuhkeu said nothing in response to their questions, his mind bent on what it was Pog had taken, which sat hidden in his quiver.

Dasemunkepeuc
Keeta Stays Behind and Tells a Story

"Ship," said Auwepu, laughing at how the strange word rolled her lips together.

"Ship," echoed Mese, baring his teeth and chasing after some of the younger ones, so that they screamed in mock fright. Keeta smiled at the ruckus but she held her gaze on the line of canoes as they made their way from Roanoke Island to the ship rocking gently in the bay. Auwepu tapped her and Keeta reluctantly retreated inland, to the growing corn and ripening melons.

"What fun it would be to visit the big canoe!" said Mese as he kicked the sand.

Keeta remembered another hot and windless day when she had run from her weeding to the shore, to what she thought was a more attractive task. "I heard they smell like angry skunks," she said. "The stink's so strong you have to cover your face with a mask of mint in order to breathe."

"Really?" asked Mese, doubtful.

"And they don't eat," added Keeta, "especially not juicy, warm melons."

Naana laughed.

"Mese," continued Keeta, "what a wonderful plan you've given me! Go gather the girls for weeding and tell them to meet us in the ancestor trees."

The boy took off. Keeta and Auwepu went to the field to search for a large, ripe melon. They carried the warm fruit back to where the ancestor trees grew tallest and the shade kept the ground cool and waited as the girls gathered. "Let's celebrate the sun and the rain and the soil for giving us this melon," said Keeta, "before we go to the fields today." The girls smiled and gathered on the soft needles. Saying a blessing of thanks, Keeta cracked the fruit open with a sharp, slanted rock and a heavy stick, and she and Auwepu passed around sweet chunks whose juices ran down their wrists while they ate.

"Tell us a story," prodded Naana.

Keeta nodded and thought of Mama, how she asked the ancestors to guide her in choosing, how she closed her eyes to gather her strength before the telling. She wiped her hands, sticky with melon, onto the cedar needles, took a breath and began.

"Our ancestors tell us that our people grew out of the death of the Great Mother. Her two sons, Nanabohzo and Malsum, used her body to make the creatures of our world. One son, Nanabohzo, kind-hearted and generous, broke off pieces of his mother to make…" She stopped here and regarded her audience, many of them still very young. "What creatures did Nanabohzo make?"

"Beaver!"

"Deer!"

"Herring!" came the shouts.

"Melon!"

"My sister!"

"Your sister? How many seasons has she seen?" said an older girl quickly. In the laughter, the one who blurted out the unfamiliar answer, her first season weeding without her mother, looked confused.

"You're putting your sister on the list of good creatures?" asked Auwepu, with a glance at Naana.

The girl nodded.

"The other son, Malsum," continued Keeta, "had hatred in his heart. He took pieces of his mother and created…

What did he create?"

"Mosquitoes!"

"Briars!"

"Snakes, like copperheads!"

"Nanabohzo grew upset at his brother's creations. He asked him to stop making such horrible animals. Malsum ignored this advice. He pushed on at an even faster pace, creating..."

"Panthers!"

"Malsum saw that to have his own way and continue making hateful creations, he must kill Nanabohzo. So he killed him by the only method possible, an owl feather."

"Why an owl?"

"Owls have always been hunters," answered Auwepu.

"Nanabohzo didn't remain dead," continued Keeta. "When he awoke he understood that he must kill Malsum, or the world would be overrun with nasty creatures. He found the one thing that could harm Malsum, a fern."

"Why a fern?"

"Because a fern is the gentlest of all things growing from the ground," said Naana, and Auwepu smiled at her sister's growing understanding of plants.

"Nanabohzo lured Malsum to the banks of a river and threw the fern at him, killing him. But Malsum, too, could not remain dead."

Keeta stopped and let the audience ponder this, that Malsum was just as strong as Nanabohzo and could not die. "Diminished, however, he slunk away and became a wolf, a creature that lives for the night. While Malsum appears to us as a wolf, Nanabohzo chose the gentlest of creatures to represent his kind and loving spirit in this world. He chose the rabbit."

Keeta gathered her strength once more, to deliver the end, a section that would probably be lost on part of her audience—the little ones had already gotten up to look in the bushes for rabbits—but was the part of the story she had pondered more and more as she grew. "My people understand that we live with both the good and the evil brother. That we have both the good and the evil brother within us, both born of the same mother. We do our best to find our balance, to reach out to the good and shun the evil, because the Creator has given us this choice."

No one spoke of it, because there was no need, because everyone with melon on their lips thought of the ship in the harbor and could think of nothing else—to which brother did these visitors belong?

Dasemunkepeuc
A New Spirit Traveler

After the last aunt had stepped safely onto the beach at
Roanoke Island, Menuhkeu made his way across the chan-
nel back to Dasemunkepeuc. Above him a soaring osprey
rode a high current. The paddle cut evenly through the calm
water. When he pulled his canoe to shore, Menuhkeu stored
it quickly on dry ground.

Although hungry, he skirted the village and walked south-
ward, toward the vast, brackish marshes. Much of the ground
was soggy, but the tide was retreating so his path would be
dry enough to pass through. Before long, Menuhkeu came
to an ancient hillock. Stashed with shells and bones, it was
the refuse of ancestors hardened into a small, dry island in
the wetland. He sat and waited. Puddles of water reflected
the orange light of the falling sun. Across the reeds a team
of ducks arched their way home for the night, landing se-
quentially, silent save the random, echoing quack.

When Pog arrived, Menuhkeu handed over the bundle without a word. Pog unwrapped the skins to reveal a
sharp-edged tool of metal, secured into a wooden handle.
Cautiously, he ran his finger along its edge. Their eyes met.
Pog grasped the handle and easily sliced through a twig.

"This is very powerful," said Pog. "I took it," he added,
answering his friend's wordless question. "The wassador
looked over all the polished shells, rolling them in his fingers,
trying them with his teeth, and then he wouldn't give this
up. When the stick went off, I took it."

Menuhkeu nodded. He didn't have to remind Pog of what

they both knew, that taking something not given was dangerous, the act's consequences unknowable. Pog sliced another
twig in half. "They were not good hosts. They didn't feed us.
They didn't understand the value of the shells."

"What will you do with it?" Menuhkeu asked at last, for
he was hungry.

"Do with it?" Pog wrapped the tool back into the skins,
careful of the sharp blade. "I'll give it to Wingina, of course."

When they returned to the village, Asku, on guard that
evening, met them with the news that Manteo had arrived
from Croatoan Island. In Manteo's hair was a crow feather,
the mark of the spirit traveler, and thrown across his shoulders lay a cape of cougar skin. The visitors were soon leaving,
Manteo had heard. They had requested that some of the
Roanoke join them in their journey home, he had heard.
And this new spirit traveler wanted to be on the ship when
it left the bay.

Dasemunkepeuc
Wanchese and Manteo Undertake a Journey

The spirit guide and healer Chepeck stood on the beach of Roanoke Island, watching the retreating figures ride up and down on the waves. The sands retained heat from the summer's day, but a cool, moist wind had kicked up and blew over Wanchese and Manteo as they were paddled out to the wassadors' ship in their square canoes. At their leaving, Chepeck had asked the Creator to guide Wanchese and Manteo. The spirit guide intoned the blessings he had been taught and then added supplications that seemed appropriate to the unforeseen situation of spirit travelers leaving by way of the sea. He had prayed, for example, that Mishibijiw the water panther would not be hungry, and that the beast would not follow the ships to the sea when his appetite returned.

Chepeck's prayers were over, but he could not take his eyes off the little canoe until Wanchese and Manteo became a blurry, slow-moving spot, the Roanoke no longer distinguishable from the wassadors.

In his watching Chepeck noticed that the light hovering over the water had shifted. Lost was the sharp, white quality it had possessed just a few days ago. Now, the sunlight shone a yellow green. When dark came, the spirit guide lifted his fist to the sky and counted upward to where the red star shone in the south. It hung low now, with its heart toward leaving. The following morning, the spirit guide went with First Mother to the fields to look at the second planting of corn. The ear they opened burst with eagerness, and he knew. He smiled, and his wrinkles widened over his thin face: it was the time of the Green Corn Festival.

Dasemunkepeuc
The Green Corn Festival

Keeta pounded the heavy oak stick into the stone mortar, grinding the corn into powder. Relieved to watch the wassador ships rock their way back through the gap and disappear into the sea, Keeta was also glad to be mashing summer corn and not winter acorns. "Will they come back?" she asked her Mama, who sat by her, husking ears.

"We didn't expect them in the first place," Mama answered, gathering up the corn silk.

Later in the quiet hours of the evening, Keeta asked her father, "Will Wanchese come back?"

Adchaen hadn't visited the wassadors' ship. Most of Dasemunkepeuc's warriors had stayed in the village as a precaution. He had seen them, though, on the beach as Wanchese made his first foray onto their canoe. "Ask me another question," he answered her. "One that I can answer."

"OK," she laughed. "Will I dance at the Green Corn Festival?"

Adchaen had been blessed with many strong children by his first wife, a capable woman from the weasel clan, but none had been like his one Keeta, daughter of his second wife of the herring clan, shiny and full of life and, at the same time, hard to keep hold of. He pondered his daughter's question; to dance meant to be ready for marriage, and a girl like his Keeta wouldn't dance for more than one season.

Mama caught her husband's hesitation. "Lucky for the tribe that when you dance, you can't also ask questions!" she teased.

* * *

And so it was that First Mother arrived the next day holding an ear of ripe corn with its tassels braided, for Keeta. First Mother chanted the blessings of the Creator and the ancestors and Keeta accepted the offering, head bowed. First Mother's voice shushed like an undercurrent as two squirrels shrieked and fought in the pine nearby, a busy crow cawed, and the boys two lodges over shouted at play. Keeta knew they were all singing to her, telling her this time was a great blessing.

Within days, on warm winds families arrived from Croatoan and Roanoke Islands, and makeshift lodgings sprouted along the river as every home had visitors. Wingina and First Mother hosted their cousin Granganimeo, his wife, Kautantowit, and their relatives.

The family of Adchaen's first wife from Croatoan Island arrived, many of them members of her weasel clan. They brought with them their warrior traditions. Before long the small children hung moss on the nearest tree for target practice and wrestled in the pine needles. Keeta welcomed the ruckus, for these weasel cousins had taught her the same games when she was younger, and she was stronger for it.

These activities lessened after a few days passed and the fast began. Keeta and Mama and the cousins had prepared their feast—the dried fish and meat, berries and corn, greens from the soft forests and verdant swamps—and put it away, for they would not eat from now until after the ceremonies. The next morning, the sun brooded red in the east and the songbirds announced the new day, and the Roanoke came together.

Bathing with the others in the place where the river slows, Keeta watched the silver ripples drop from her gourd and race down her thigh, the water making streams down her leg to rejoin the mother river. The chilled water raised her skin and set her blood moving. When she was cleansed, Mama handed Keeta her new skirt. She had sewn the blue flowers smaller, but woven-corn-silk tassels danced along the bottom, intricate decorations that would probably not last the day. Then Keeta sat while Mama braided more corn silk into her hair. They rested quietly by the river, glad for a spell to be away from the noisy weasel cousins and to listen to the water run over the rocks before they rejoined the festivities.

To commence the feast, the weroance Wingina offered appowac to the Creator. He threw a handful in each of the four directions that bring the wind, so that the blessings would follow Wanchese and Manteo and all the Roanoke people wherever they went.

From the outskirts leapt the dancers. Shaking their gourds and rattling the shells tied to their arms and legs, they surrounded the crowd. Keeta felt the beat in her heart and stamped out the rhythm, as they all did, until the circle was formed. The stamping led to a chanting, led by Chepeck. Keeta threw her own voice into the voices of those around her, the ground rocked with their feet, and she felt herself grow closer to the sky.

When the sun had crossed the midpoint and the voices were hoarse, Chepeck called in the warriors.

Cleansed and painted, the warriors shouted out, their voices one, deep and powerful. Up they reached, as if to take an arrow and shoot it, and then down, as if bent low with a hatchet, until their palms touched the ground and beat out a rhythm. Circling, they twisted, the older ones in front and at the end the youngest warriors, those who had made their moon trek just a year ago. In the jangling excitement Keeta searched for and found Menuhkeu. She could not help but watch his every move, as he bent low, as he reached back as if to take an arrow and shoot it. Down and up they went, over and over, until sweat made them slick. Not a flashy dancer, Menuhkeu made no extra moves, but in his steadiness he conveyed his strength. Pog knew to turn his elbow for effect as he pulled his bow and to bend his knees in two beats as he hit the ground, and Keeta watched him as well, as did many others, but with a different feeling in her heart.

The warriors then danced a hunt to thank the Creator for the bounty taken by the Roanoke for their survival. Poor Moskeke! Many years he had played the deer. Covered in a full skin, a head with large antlers masking his own face and four hooves rattling along the ground, he wove among the warriors who hit at him with their heavy clubs or shot their headless arrows, in their dance sometimes forgetting that it was Moskeke underneath.

When Moskeke lay motionless, abandoned by the warrior dancers, the dancing women, clapping and stomping into a line, called in a low, repetitive chant. Keeta watched First Mother, then Kautantowit from Roanoke Island, and then Wequassus, mother of Menuhkeu and the most graceful dancer in all the villages. Her hand fell just so on her palm as she clapped, her face calm and without distraction. The women embraced the tribe with their trilling song, a song of corn and beans and melons and plenty. As they danced the setting sun sent long shadows through the pines. When their song became quieter and quieter, Keeta felt a pull on her elbow, Auwepu. "Come on," she whispered, "it's nearly our time." Her friend's face, so beautiful, so calm, revealed the opposite of what Keeta felt. This was the moment, Keeta knew, and she barely had the time to hold onto this experience of expectation, so quickly was she pulled into the group to perform.

Keeta, Auwepu, and four other girls from Dasemunkepeuc as well as three girls from Roanoke Island and seven who had traveled from Croatoan, gathered in the center of the meeting circle. Facing inward toward each other, they raised their arms to the sky in supplication and thanks to the Creator for their lifeblood. Their feet found the same heartbeat, their bodies swayed as if in a light breeze. There had been no need to practice the corn dance—girls dance these steps from the time their feet leave their mother's carriers and hit the ground. It is the dance of life, the dance of gratitude. Graceful Auwepu was able to make her arms and her hips twirl like the wind circling dry leaves, and Keeta saw quite a few warriors watching her friend as she brought her palms to the side of her head like a fan and floated them upwards. As they found their voices and turned outward to the tribe, Keeta felt the watching on her. She gathered it to her, to draw strength, unconcerned whose eyes were on her, searching in her heart only for the Creator, found in all living things.

When the full moon rose over the ancestor trees in the east, the corn dancers lowered their voices, slowed their steps, and made their way away from the gathering, toward the trees. This was how it had always been done. Keeta turned from the fire and looked into the growing dark. The girls separated and Keeta, now alone, quickened her step as she approached the old cedars, moving almost at a run as her feet hit the familiar soft bedding of the forest.

The moonlight sliced through the forest and the trunks glowed silver. She heard the laughter of the tribe at the fire as the women gathered the food for the feast that would last for many hours. She should turn back now, as was expected, but it was all so beautiful—the shadows, the moon, the beating of her heart as it slowed and rested after her dancing.

Then it happened. A warm, familiar hand grabbed hers. She turned and faced Menuhkeu. His face barely visible through his fading paint, she recognized at once his touch, his scent. She was surprised and not surprised to find him suddenly here with her. "I have something for you," he said. "If you'll take it."

He let go her hand and pulled up his gift, a large blanket,

stitched entirely of rabbit skins. She reached out, felt its heaviness in her hands and brought the soft fur to her face. She looked at Menuhkeu. "Yes," she said. "Yes, I will."

"Where have you been?" Keeta's cousin asked, his high, young voice unable to whisper. "You missed the cinnamon water."

"Shush," his mother whispered.

Don't these weasel cousins ever rest? thought Keeta, who had hoped to come back to her lodging unnoticed, or at least unremarked on.

A second hand that evening reached out to grab hers, her Mama. Keeta knelt by her mother's skins, where she once also had slept. Mama caressed her face with her open palm, kissed her forehead. "I know which one I want," said Keeta as quietly as she could, although she knew every ear in the lodging was perked. She showed Mama her gift, the large blanket of rabbit skins.

Expert sewer that she was, Mama turned the blanket over to examine the workmanship. She ran her finger over the careful stitching and felt the fullness of the skins. "Mmm," Mama replied. "You don't have to keep the first fish you catch."

Keeta sunk her fingers in the fur. "I've only ever wanted the same fish."

"Wanting one fish makes it easy, then." Mama handed the blanket back to her daughter. "I think your friend Auwepu caught a net full."

Dasemunkepeuc
Keeta Visits Rikopqua to Be Inked

The inker Rikopqua shared a tiny lodging close to the river
with her sister Wautog, the woman who was a friend to the
plants. Roanoke girls and women had relied on Rikopqua's
discerning eye and steady hand for many years. Rikopqua
saved her talents for the girls. She did not ink the boys.
Boys were inked when they became young warriors, after
completing their moon trek. Then a boy received Wingina's
mark—four arrows across the right shoulder.

A girl was first inked when she became a wife, small oval
links on her upper right arm that looped in a circle. First
Mother had the additional inkings of diamond nets on her
thighs to reflect her status as keeper of the corn.

Keeta had fasted, and Mama fingered walnut oil through
her hair with a small-toothed comb of ash wood. She rubbed
oil onto her daughter's skin until it shone.

Rikopqua had lifted the window flaps at one corner of the
dwelling, and the yellow fall light warmed her workspace.
Against the far wall Auwepu rested, her arm in poultices.
Three women from her new family, shell polishers of great
repute, sat silently by her. Auwepu's mother had gone over
to the world of the dead a long time ago. Although Naana
was too young to accompany her sister to be inked, she had
still managed to be present, to help Wautog, she said, in
preparing the poultices.

Auwepu brightened and smiled to see Keeta and Naana
came over to touch her arm in hello. Auwepu's soon-to-be-
husband, Aquandut, came from a line of bear clan women

from Roanoke Island, the kind of people who were slow to welcome, yet fierce in protecting those already welcomed in.

Auwepu's new relatives remained seated, giving quiet, polite greetings to Keeta and Mama when, with a flourish, in came Wequassus, Menuhkeu's mother, of the crane clan. Even if the bear clan women didn't recognize her at once as the wife of one Wingina's most trusted warriors and a member of the most prestigious clan, the long strand of pearls from each ear would have indicated her status, which is why she wore the glittering nacre at every opportunity. Once the hierarchy was established, Wequassus threw her charms about like a spring wind spreading apple blossoms.

Auwepu and Mama laughed at her light chatter, and Naana was pulled into a warm embrace. Even the heavy faces of the bear clan women broke into smiles. Wequassus saved her best compliments for Keeta, the girl who knew how many melons would grow in a field before the seeds were planted, the girl who had captured her son in her clever net.

Rikopqua waited patiently until the time had come to do what they had gathered for. The inking woman had set out thick seating mats, and over a small fire she brewed a medicinal tea. She handed Keeta a gourd to drink. In a clear voice, Rikopqua chanted. She asked the Creator to guide her. After each blessing Rikopqua called out, the women in the lodge answered affirmations in low voices. Rikopqua then asked the Creator to guide Keeta in her marriage. She asked the Creator to help Keeta to count her corn accurately, to aid her in giving birth with courage, and to protect Keeta's children from poisonous plants and hungry panthers. Out of a simmering clay pot, Rikopqua removed a heated poultice scented with wapeih, as well as other plants and roots that were harder to recognize. Almost as soon as the hot compress met Keeta's arm, her skin went to sleep.

The tea had calmed her as well. Wequassus wisely gave up

the closest seat to Mama, who said nothing but sat with her thigh against her daughter's. Rikopqua took Keeta's arm in her thin, cold hands. She removed the poultice and began the process, using thorns dipped in ink made from ingredients known only to Rikopqua and those she chose to teach her art. She worked with precision and energy, each prick quick and deep, stopping only to clean whatever blood dripped down.

Keeta felt each pierce, and there were many. The tea urged her inward, to put some distance between her thoughts and the thorns, but more palliative than the tea was the gentle gossip among the women, trading stories of the two villages.

At the end, her arm was wrapped in warm poultices, which would be changed regularly until the red wounds lost their anger. Keeta and Auwepu looked at each other from across the lodge, each now with a bandaged arm, each seated with new family. When their arms healed, they each would be married.

Dasemunkepeuc
Meeting at the Hillock, and Keeta is Welcomed by Her New Family

Keeta and Menuhkeu had met at the hillock in the great marsh just after their marriage, seeking privacy from crowded lodges and prying relatives. Straddling water and land, the great marsh never rested. Birds, fish, and plants of all kinds made their home just here, not on the ocean, not in the forests nearby. Washed back and forth by the tides, at times it was impassable and at times a person who knew the paths could make their way across to the dry inland. The hillock, in the open and so often windswept, also benefited from the warm fall sun. Menuhkeu and Keeta found this small dry spot a perfect place to be together.

Menuhkeu had long been drawn to Keeta, but he hadn't expected that, once he had reeled her in, the way she held him in her gaze would loosen his lips. He found himself talking to her more than he spoke to anyone else, the things close to his heart bubbling up one after the other as he wanted her to understand the things he had seen. They talked of what had happened on the stranger's ship, and of what Pog had taken. "The handle is smooth wood, but the tool is metal and very sharp. So sharp it draws blood, like the tip of an arrow. So that if I did this," he made a chopping motion across his thigh, "my skin would open up and I might lose my leg."

Keeta took his hand and held it while she thought about what he had said. "But not copper?" she asked, recounting. "Something much stronger."

"Asku used this tool to dress a deer and he was done way

ahead of Kelchis." Menuhkeu frowned.

"Really!" Keeta tried to picture this.

"Kelchis is still angry about being bested. He claims that a tool that lets you do the steps too quickly is dangerous because you don't have time to thank the Creator as you work."

A lone harrier flew low over the brown grasses, prowling for food.

"Could this tool be faster than the hatchets we have for cutting down trees and limbs to make the lodges?"

Menuhkeu knew that Keeta, as she grew, had been discussed by the elders for the way her thoughts carried so swiftly. This quality of hers still caught him by surprise each time. It made him proud as he worked to catch up to her. "Yes..."

"Wouldn't it be better to find this out as well? To understand everything this new tool can do? Then when Wanchese returns perhaps we can trade with more knowledge of what we can get from these strangers."

"Instead of worrying about what they can take."

The fall sun lowered and a chill fell. Soon the tide would rise and it would difficult to return to the village. Keeta took back her hand and reluctantly stood to go. How quickly she had given over her heart. How quickly he had become hers, and she his.

"Do it again, Keeta," said Minneash, hands resting on her wide belly, full to bursting with a child. "Show us again how you keep so close an eye."

Keeta sighed, frustrated. "It's not that hard," she replied. "As long as you know what pieces you need to make a whole picture." She pulled her stick through the hard ground. "Let's say this is the field." She drew a circle. "And this is where the sun comes up." She looked up at her new sister-in-law and wondered, not for the first time, how Owush, a warrior of great standing, could have married a woman so unskilled at keeping track of her crops.

"Begin with the first corn harvest in a dry year," continued Keeta, now aware that the others in the lodging were listening to their discussion. "In the field closest to the river, the one to the north of the swamp." Her new family was intrigued that Keeta was praised for her ability to keep track of the crops and to predict the stores throughout the winter. Her new sister wanted to know her secret. In Keeta's mind there was no secret—First Mother had taught her since she had been a small girl, and her Mama had long consulted her about what they might have left over for trade.

"A dry year means less corn," said Minneash and she gave her belly a pat. "That I know."

"A dry year means fewer acorns as well," said Keeta. "And the acorns may be smaller and the animals more aggressive in taking them for their own. And so..."

"And so less left over for trading," put in Wequassus, with an emphasis that concluded the conversation. Wequassus, whose name meant swan, found her best pleasure in sharing news. This meant she was also adroit at finding it. She regarded the village as a basket of intricate design, and when one strand of reed was pulled, she relished knowing which of the others would move.

Having reclaimed the talk, Wequassus twisted her dried vines into a thin rope while her daughters-in-law waited for her to continue. "I hear," she said at last, her voice as always pleasant and inviting. "That some aunts on Roanoke Island received a great prize from the wassadors, in exchange for some melons."

It was joked in Dasemunkepeuc that on Roanoke, the source of all polished shells in the area, all newborn babies must learn to trade smiles for their mother's milk, so proficient were they at negotiating.

Keeta, by way of Naana, knew that Auwepu's new family had acquired a copper bowl. Auwepu had laughed at the fuss, saying that food cooked in it had a strange and unpleasant aftertaste.

"It would be a gracious and right gesture if we could at least see these new things," Wequassus continued.

Keeta merely nodded. If Wequassus knew that Keeta could find her a copper bowl, her mother-in-law would not rest until she had it in her hands. Keeta made a show of turning back to her calculations of the corn, but her mind was troubled. A copper pot was nothing in comparison to what Pog had taken and given to Wingina, according to Menuhkeu's description. The power in that tool was worth any number of copper pots. She felt her new mother's eye weighing her.

"Minneash," said Keeta as nonchalantly as she could muster. "Which animal spirit would best protect your baby— bobcat for stealth, hawk for hunting, or fox for adaptability?"

At the other end of the lodge, Wampeikuc gave his son an approving glance. The boy had won an excellent wife.

Dasemunkepeuc and Pomeioc
Wingina and His Council Consider an Invitation

Menuhkeu stepped out of his lodge and pulled the flap
back tight to seal in the heat. In the stillness, he looked to
the stars of the winter-maker glinting above, three in a row,
crisp and white. Ahead, at the other end of the village, the
shifting blaze of the fire circle danced. He strode in that direction, where Wingina had called a council to discuss a recent
invitation from a new weroance of a nearby Secotan village.

The flames rose in orange and yellow. Those who didn't
sit around the fire stood or sat just beyond, listening, ready,
some wrapped in heavy skins against the chill. Menuhkeu
stood with the younger warriors.

Wingina wore his skin of a black bear. The animal's powerful fur climbed up the weroance's back, its pointed face
perched above Wingina's like a guardian. This skin had been
his grandfather's, who was a weroance before him and whose
bones lay wrapped in deerskin in the tombs of the elders.

"The Secotan weroance has lost the strength of his grip
on his allies." Wampeikuc recounted the background, as he
often did at council. "And Peimacum, this new weroance of
Pomeioc village, has reached out to us, on his own."

A low whistle announced the approach of a friend. Out
of the darkness appeared Granganimeo of Roanoke Island,
recognizable by his broad frame and rambling gait. As he
approached, two young warriors rose and stood outside the
fire to give him room. Granganimeo settled in to the right
of Wingina and was offered food from the clay pot warming
in the embers of the fire.

Granganimeo ate, and they waited. It appeared that Peimacum had broken his allegiance with the Secotan weroance and wanted to meet, apart from the Secotan alliance, with the Roanoke. This invitation demanded an immediate answer and so the council met.

After Granganimeo had eaten, Wingina tossed a handful of appowac into the flames to rebalance the council after the newcomer's arrival. In his low, calm tones Wingina laid out the crux of the problem—with the gift of the run of herring and sturgeon often came jealous trouble, this time from Peimacum, whose Pomeioc was the closest Secotan village.

"Perhaps the new weroance wants access to the Roanoke fishing areas and shellfish beds," added Wampeikuc.

A few older warriors murmured in agreement.

"With that access, this Peimacum could move to become the new weroance of all the Secotan," concluded Wampeikuc.

Menuhkeu watched the faces both at the fire and those standing just outside it turn toward his father, listening and nodding. Wampeikuc was known for his understanding of what others would want from the Roanoke, and this distrust of the motives of outsiders served the tribe well. Menuhkeu wondered if his brother Owush, who grew every day to look more and more like his father, would take on this teaching role. His eyes turned to his father-in-law, Adchaen, who was respected as a warrior and a hunter but rarely spoke in council. "The Creator has given me many gifts," he once explained around the fire, after a hunt. "I don't seek the gifts of others."

Ensenore, the oldest of the Roanoke people, pulled his thin arm out from under his blanket of fox skins. Two paws dangled at his wrist, casting a wriggling shadow on the ground behind him. "Old weroance, new weroance, we can't choose for the Secotan. We need only get along with our neighbors." Implicit in Ensenore's brief comment was the understanding that the greater enemies lay to the north and west of them in the Powhatan and the Mangoak. The wassador visitors from the sea, who had taken Wanchese and Manteo and not yet returned, went unmentioned, but their presence lurked, like the shadows that moved in the trees just outside the fire.

Kelchis, his choppy cadence and his point of view so familiar that some need hear only the rhythm of his speech to know that he spoke of enemies, of danger, muttered for all to hear, "Those in Pomeioc have long been jealous of our bounty."

The fire crackled and the forest shifted in the light wind.

"What news from Croatoan?" Wingina asked Granganimeo, who had just returned from there.

Granganimeo, his voice loud and jovial, assured Wingina that the people of Croatoan would join in what Wingina decided, such was their respect for his judgment and such was the strength of their alliance.

"Now that Peimacum has made an offer, not to consider it would be an aggressive act," commented the spirit guide Chepeck in his rabbit cloak.

Menuhkeu felt the shift in the people at these words. He and Asku exchanged a quick glance. They and some of the others whose markings were three years old or less had never gone to another village as warriors and were eager to test themselves and visit these neighbors.

Wingina's face registered this shift as well. The will of the people for peace had guided him for many years. He nodded. "We must meet this Peimacum," he said. "We will travel to Pomeioc. But won't go unaware, nor unarmed. In fact," he added, "we will bring the powerful wassador tool to increase our advantage." With that he held up the sharp tool that by now had been handled and appreciated by all present. The group voiced its assent. They would go, and they would bring the tool.

Later that evening, wrapped in their rabbit blanket, Keeta asked Menuhkeu question after question. Didn't the Secotan have their own shellfish beds, how many herring were left over to trade away, who was this Peimacum to claim his own rights? "Keeta," Menuhkeu finally told her, "you need to go to council yourself. I'm done telling you what happened."

She turned away from him and laughed. "What?" he whispered. "What's so funny?"

"You," she answered softly, turning back to him. "You thinking that you can resist my questions."

Pomeioc
The Roanoke Travel to Pomeioc

Pomeioc lay a half-day's travel south of Dasemunkepeuc. The painted warriors left their village as one, the scouts in the front, followed by Wampeikuc and then Wingina, all moving quickly, almost at a run.

At a meeting spot down the trail, the Dasemunkepeuc warriors were joined by those of Granganimeo from Roanoke Island and others from Croatoan, seventy-four warriors in total.

The day was cold and bright and blue. Menuhkeu, marching near Asku and Pog, worked to quiet his anticipation of this first foray against a potentially dangerous tribe since he had become a warrior. Wingina had long ruled by negotiation, aided by his cousin Granganimeo, whose control of the polished shells garnered him wide respect along the coast. "Now I can prove myself," Pog confided after they had travelled a while. Pog, whose family wasn't as prominent as Menuhkeu's, wanted evidence of his strength to win a wife.

As they neared Pomeioc their pace slowed, so that the Roanoke visitors would enter their host's territory with the proper presence of mind. "Why haven't we been greeted?" muttered Asku. Neither Menuhkeu nor Pog had an answer. No party approached any part of Roanoke territory without being met by warriors, to guide them to the village as guests or to intercept.

As the warriors well knew, the approach to Dasemunkepeuc was a gradual path to the center of their village—from the sea a path through the ancestor trees, from the land a path through the swamps and then fields, until arriving at the feast areas, the homes, the temple and the death lodge.

The contrast in the approach to Pomeioc took the younger warriors by surprise. The friends exchanged questioning glances when they reached the fallow winter fields and saw the outskirts of the village.

A high fence of closely placed, pointed stakes curled around the entire village, the entrance a twisting corridor. Slight gaps in the stakes revealed slivers of the buildings inside. No one, not even a small child, could squeeze his way through the narrow gaps.

Wingina halted the march, to wait and greet the Pomeioc.

Nine Pomeioc warriors appeared, their faces in the blue and red of Peimacum's men. They took their long bows and made a ceremony of laying them in a pile before they approached.

Peimacum emerged. Much younger than Wingina and new to his position, he strode forcefully. His wide chest swung. Menuhkeu couldn't help but contrast Peimacum's carriage to Wingina's long, thin legs and narrow, graceful frame.

A warrior with two red cardinal feathers hanging from his hair took a pipe from the pouch that hung at his side and tamped in a generous portion of appowac. The pipe was long and made of black clay. He lit it from a burning stick and took a deep breath before he passed it to Wingina, who also drew deeply at the stem. The pipe was passed among the elder warriors and then Wingina turned to his men to signal that it was time to visit the village.

As the Roanoke moved toward the entrance, Wingina called to Menuhkeu. "You will wait here for the others," he said, "and let us know when they have arrived."

Menuhkeu held in his excitement at being singled out by his leader as worthy of responsibility and nodded his assent.

"Take a companion who won't let you fall asleep," Wingina added. The joke worked its magic, as the Pomeioc laughed and teased the younger warrior, so unskilled that he was left outside.

Menuhkeu nodded to Asku to stay and then to Pog, who turned the sharp corner into Pomeioc and disappeared with the rest of the Roanoke warriors, leaving Menuhkeu and Asku on their own.

Silent for a long while as they stood, they waited for no one, for no other warriors were expected. Wingina had entrusted them with the important task of staying, watching.

Time passed and the rhythmic thumps of hands beating the ground and chanting reached them. Later the pungent smell of cooking wafted their way.

"Maybe," commented Asku, "this Peimacum is offering a feast in friendship."

"I guess we're having a wassador feast, then."

Asku laughed at this. A wassador feast had come to mean no feast at all among the younger warriors, after the trading party had ended with everyone hungry.

When the afternoon turned its face toward evening, a brown hare made its way in the frozen hillocks of the barren cornfields. The animal went up on his hind legs, sniffed the air and retreated back into the stubble. Menuhkeu glanced at Asku, he had seen it too. Had Nanabohzo, the great trickster hare, sent them a sign?

Menuhkeu turned and peered between the staves, into Pomeioc. The slanted, late sun made long, dark stripes of shade of the fence, and the striations of light and dark blurred Menuhkeu's view. It occurred to him that Nanabohzo wouldn't stay in one place, visible for all to see, for as many hours as he and Asku had.

Menuhkeu tilted his head to indicate he would walk the perimeter of the fence. Silently but careful not to give the impression of sneaking, he moved quickly so as to appear as just a passing shadow to anyone who happened to glance outward.

Out over the marsh, a team of ducks headed in for the evening. Abruptly, they reversed course, sending up a cacophony of quacking. Something had startled them from their regular landing spot. Menuhkeu stopped and looked toward the swamp. Far in the distance he caught a movement in the trees and he saw it—a group of women and small children moving away from the village. He knew at once that if the women and their children were leaving the village, something was amiss inside the staves.

He gave the warning call of the screech owl as he returned to Asku, who repeated the warning call.

Within a few seconds Menuhkeu and Asku heard the unmistakable whooping and calling sounds of a fight. "The gate," said Menuhkeu, and they readied arrows in their bows and moved into the instantly confining, twisting entrance, their vision laced by thin strips of shadow and light. A few turns in, they saw the red-and-blue backs of two Pomeioc guards moving inward to meet the fleeing Roanoke.

Menuhkeu and Asku let go their arrows. Menuhkeu's went into the back thigh of the guard on the left, and Asku's hit the warrior to the right. The felled men dropped to the ground, blood flowing down their legs, just as the first of the Roanoke came into sight. Menuhkeu and Asku turned the narrow exit to their advantage by holding it and shooting their arrows at the pursuing Pomeioc, turning what would have been a crucible into a protected path.

Pog, leading the retreat, reached his friends and turned to join them in securing a Roanoke escape.

As they later learned, there were several Pomeioc injuries, but the most severely hurt was Peimacum. Adchaen, not hesitating at Menuhkeu's warning of trickery, had turned to Peimacum with the wassador tool and gored his thigh.

While the arrows still flew Wampeikuc hurried out through

the exit, Wingina at his side, the two fleeing into the woods at great speed.

When the last of the Roanoke had left, Menuhkeu and Asku turned and fled as well, Pog at the rear. The Pomeioc hesitated just long enough at their own exit to allow the three to make it to the woods unharmed.

They were not followed.

Menuhkeu took his place in a long line of warriors as they raced toward home before dark fell. The whole incident had taken a mere few moments but that short time had already created a large gap of before and after in his mind. Menuhkeu had received a sign from Nanabohzo and had acted in a way that helped his people.

Later that evening the men of the tribe would nod to him in respect, and they would ask him to tell them the story. By then this new feeling would sit more comfortably, but for most of the way home Menuhkeu went over the sight of the hare in the field and how he had known to look toward the swamp, how he had received the messages from the ducks, and then how he had seen the retreating Pomeioc women, elders, and children. He felt that each step had been a hint, a whisper that he could have easily missed. This understanding terrified him until he resolved to be more thankful of and observe more carefully the signs the Creator sends to all creatures. Only then did the events cohere into a narrative, into a story he could tell when asked, "How did you know to warn us just as the Pomeioc were reaching for their bows and clubs?"

When safely far away from Pomeioc, the Roanoke stopped to put oak leaf compresses on the wounded. None were so hurt that they couldn't be carried on the backs of others, and the party made it back to Dasemunkepeuc before the winter-maker rose high in the sky.

Dasemunkepeuc
First Mother Teaches Keeta about Trading

The days quietly shed their light, and the soil tightened into itself.

Throughout the summer, the women had gathered green plants, melons, and soft berries. In the fall, they secured corn, beans, acorns and hickory nuts in tightly woven baskets and placed them deep in the earth. They layered the lodge mats tightly against the coming cold. The men had hauled in the nets and weirs and turned to hunting.

Brown leaves littered the ground, and the wind held its breath as Keeta ventured out into the early gray light to her Mama's lodge. The brush rustled. Panther had been seen lurking near the big marsh, so Keeta raised the large stick she carried. She slowed her pace. A red squirrel twittered. At this, Keeta laughed and twittered a return. Shortly ahead, she espied Naana kneeling near some mushrooms thriving underneath a gnarled oak.

"It's my hunting season too," Naana said in greeting. As Wautog aged and since her sister Auwepu had married and gone to Roanoke Island, Naana had taken over more and more of the healer's duties.

Keeta sat while her friend worked her small shell tool around the base of the tan, rounded plants. "What do you hear of your sister?" Keeta asked.

"She is well along, like you."

"If they're boys, our children will go on their moon trek together."

Naana loosened a mushroom, careful to preserve the stem,

and thanking the plant, she dropped it into her basket. The girl's sadness at missing her sister was the tribe's gain. Naana's energy and knowledge about healing plants had increased rapidly in Auwepu's absence, but Keeta knew that to mention this would be unkind. "Naana," she said instead. "Let me ask you a question."

Naana looked up, taken by Keeta's tone.

"You have seen the sharp tool?"

Naana nodded. Everyone had seen it, had heard the story of how the new object had kept the Secotan weroance afraid. Most had tried it, for one task or another.

"Would a tool like that be helpful to you, in your work with Wautog?"

Naana frowned as she considered this. "Maybe to loosen the earth around deep roots. But the medicine plants… they give themselves to us and we thank them. We do not take them. We don't need such force." She brightened. "For making mats, though, yes, it would be helpful to take more reeds more quickly! And to take the branches for the lodge supports!"

They both laughed at the thought of it, the trouble they went to, to gather enough reeds for their roof mats, to find the strong, narrow trees for their homes.

The wind gusted. Keeta stood up. "Panther is prowling," she warned. "Be on the look-out."

Keeta's Mama's lodge was warm with a fire burning low in the center, its smoke wending up through the vent in the ceiling. Three toddlers were playing a rolling-around game as she arrived. One by one they shyly came over to say hello to the child growing inside her. "They're closest to remembering what it was like, coming from the spirit world," commented Mama. "Their messages are often heard, and remembered."

Keeta accepted the children's greetings, but her thoughts

wandered elsewhere. "I hope I'm able to learn well what First Mother is coming to teach me." She sat on the long, skin-covered bench that ran the length of the lodge.

"It's time for her to pass it on, and she has chosen you. That is enough."

First Mother's brusque hello interrupted them, as her wide shoulders twisted their way through the flaps. Although her energy remained robust and hearty, gray had crept into her hair.

First Mother waved away a cup of hot sassafras, sat and took Keeta's hands in hers. She closed her eyes, and they waited for a moment, their stillness causing even the toddlers to stop their play. "We ask the Creator for guidance in this teaching," she intoned, "to clear our minds and make sharp the etchings of our memories." She reached into her pouch for a sharp stick and settled onto the floor.

Keeta felt First Mother's strength and relaxed into it.

"First, I will show you where we are, so you will know how others see us. This," First Mother said, dragging a crooked line on the ground, "is where our Roanoke lands meet the bay. "This is where we are now—Dasemunkepeuc." She marked in the dirt the three arrows that also mark the backs of the Roanoke warriors. She pointed east of Dasemunkepeuc. "This is the bay." Her stick working, she drew a circle in the bay and put three arrows inside it. "This is Roanoke Island, and this," three more arrows appeared in a circle south of Roanoke Island, "is Croatoan."

"What's over there?" asked Keeta, pointing the empty place to the east.

"The sea."

Keeta shifted the changing weight of her body and watched First Mother, how her strong fingers lightly held the shaft of the oak and how her hair hung loosely over her face, which was concentrated on the markings.

"Is this where the marshes are?" Keeta asked, pointing to a spot just below and west of Dasemunkepeuc.

First Mother nodded. "See how far inland they go." Another crooked line became the Moratuk River that flowed down from the mountains, far to the west. Much closer, a square stood for the closest enemy, the village of Pomeioc.

She rubbed the markings out and handed Keeta the stick. Keeta redrew the lines. As she worked, she matched the markings to what she knew. She thought of the wet edge of the sand as it hit the bay, of Auwepu on Roanoke Island, of the spirit traveler Manteo from Croatoan, and of the tool her father had used on the weroance of Pomeioc.

Mama took the babies outside to breathe the fresh air and catch some of the sunshine that had begun to break in the west. First Mother continued. "Here," she made more distant marks, "are the lands of our allies, the Secotan, the Weapemeok, and the Choanoak." She added three circles, the last very large. These names too, Keeta had heard, but it was harder for her to draw them again, since she had no pictures in her mind to match.

After the Roanoke allies, First Mother drew the position of powerful distant neighbors with whom the Roanoke had little contact—the Mangoak, who lived far to the west and were known for their copper trading and violent warriors, and the Powhatan, who lived to the north and had the repu-tation of seeking always to expand their influence.

Keeta copied. First Mother erased. "Watch again, daugh-ter," she said gently. The head of a large wolf skin hung over the bench just behind her. As a very young girl Keeta had pulled on its ears, lifting up the thick, gray fur of its head, playing that she was a real wolf running through the crinkled leaves of fall in search of food, calling to Mama to rejoin her people. This last part especially made Mama laugh, because herring clan people are easily eaten by wolves.

Keeta took the stick from First Mother's hand and tried once more. When she was done, First Mother nodded and sat back. "Can you close your eyes," she asked, "and see what you have drawn in the dirt?"

Keeta closed her eyes—the blue bay sparkled, the Moratuk River ran into the interior, and the villages appeared one by one. Keeta saw herself traveling through them, journeying there and back again. She opened her eyes.

"Inside your mind," First Mother said, "you have a pattern, like the veins of a leaf. Now you can use that pattern to think and to plan."

"Plan for what, First Mother?"

"First to safeguard the food we grow, to feed our people. To know what we have that we can trade away without starving ourselves."

Keeta nodded. This she understood.

"Some years we could use some extra squash. Some years we have more beans than we need. I travel with Wingina on the trading parties because I know what we have and what we can spare. Wingina, Granganimeo, they need that knowledge so that they can trade with ease. I have that, and the understanding of how they trade, what they need. Soon you will understand as well. I want you to accompany the next trading party, to see and to learn."

The laughing of the children just outside echoed faintly and Keeta unconsciously brought her hands to her rounded belly. She recalled her Mama's words, "she has chosen you. That is enough." At her back, Keeta felt the familiar pulling, as if a hard shell were growing. She nodded at First Mother. She knew she could do this, all the questions forming in her mind as she listened.

Dasemunkepeuc, Weapemeok Territory
Keeta and Menuhkeu Journey With the Trading Party

Keeta fastened the new medicine bag to her belt. A line of polished shells scalloped the bottom of the small deerskin pouch, sewn in intricate stitches by her Mama. These valuable blue-tinted beads reflected her status, and served as well as a private reminder of the blue myrtle she had worn as a child. Inside the pouch sat a herring clan totem—the bones of an ancient fish pressed into a flat black rock.

Blanket and ground corn packed, Keeta was ready to leave.

Minneash passed her wriggling infant, Pishpesh, to Keeta. The new mother made as if she needed to free her hands to pack a pad of moss onto the carrying board before she settled the baby into the harness, but Minneash really wanted to give Keeta the baby's blessings before her journey.

"He'll pee all over your dinner," laughed Wequassus.

The joke neatly covered the women's sadness at Keeta's leaving, as befitted Wequassus's skills as a hostess, smoothing every uneven edge. "We will miss you while you travel, daughter."

Menuhkeu stepped quickly into the lodge and interrupted Keeta's response. "We're waiting."

Keeta handed the baby back to his mother. "Don't grow too much when I'm gone," she told him. "I don't want to come back and find you already a warrior."

The weak sun sparkled slightly on the choppy waters as three large canoes and two smaller ones of twenty Roanoke headed first north and then westward into the broad sound, toward the Moratuk River.

Included with Keeta and Menuhkeu from Dasemunkepeuc were Wingina, Wampeikuc, Owush, and Pog. From Roanoke Island were Granganimeo and Aquandut—Auwepu's husband and warrior from a shell-polishing family of great wealth. Asku stayed behind with Adchaen in case the Secotan took advantage or the wassadors returned. First Mother would not come because she wanted Keeta to feel the full weight of her responsibility.

Menuhkeu, in the back of a smaller canoe, paddled steadily. The wind from the northeast lost some of its bite as they traveled away from the sea. As he paddled, he scanned the shore reflexively, as his father had taught him. The flattened winter marsh, brown and gold, had sprung up bright green in the spring and early summer. Geese and ducks replaced the osprey and crane that left south with the heat. Further inland grew barrens of pine where, with luck, they would catch a good deer or two to supplement the corn meal they carried.

The first leg of the trip took them through Weapemeok territory. The Weapemeok and their weroance, Okisko, were friends of the Roanoke. The second leg would take them further into the sound, to Choanoak territory. The Choanoak weroance, the great Menatonon, controlled access to all the trade routes to the interior, and twice yearly the Roanoke traveled to trade and to offer what was due.

Menuhkeu remembered visiting the great Menatonon for the first time, how he had felt as one of a small group of red-and-yellow painted Roanoke amidst a group of seven hundred Choanoak warriors painted green and yellow. On the trip home, his father had pressed his boy for his insights. Since his older brother Owush had been traveling in another canoe, Menuhkeu had felt free to confess feeling very unimportant. Wampeikuc had surprised him by laughing out loud. "Yes!" he said. "Like one leaf on a many-limbed beech! One tiny leaf so high up that you can't even see it from the ground."

Confused, Menuhkeu had blurted out, "Why is it funny to be the little leaf? Doesn't that make us weak?"

"Stop paddling," Wampeikuc responded. "Turn around to face me."

Menuhkeu had done as he was told.

"Small in numbers is not weak," Wampeikuc had told his son. "Small in stature is not weak."

They resumed paddling. Wampeikuc had continued, "Living as we do, between the water and the land, requires special knowledge, special skills. Only those who have it will survive and prosper."

Menuhkeu lifted his paddle out of the water and looked ahead to where his father currently paddled with Wingina. The son remembered the last of his father's advice—not knowing one's strengths is one's biggest weakness. No doubt his father was talking now as he paddled, opining with the weroance on the best way to wrap an arrow or pull the innards out of a deer. This made Menuhkeu both smile and be glad that he was in the smaller canoe with his wife.

The new moon gave the travelers an advantage with the tides, and in the afternoon the canoes easily turned into the marsh, paddled over the flattened winter grass toward firmer ground, in Weapemeok territory. When Wingina gave the word, the Roanoke pulled ashore to a landing area where the banks bordered drier ground and a short path led to a stand of pine.

Pog, Owush, and Aquandut went to search out a deer. Keeta gathered brush for the couple's shelter. Pine needles and their rabbit blanket would make a soft bed.

Menuhkeu came from securing the canoes and grabbed

her hand. "Come on," he said. "Let's walk."

Keeta looked at the sky, orange in the west, already dark in the east.

"It won't take long," he encouraged.

The two headed into a deeper section of the pines and, from the bent branches and small breaks in the bushes, Keeta saw they were following a trail.

Just as the dark began to drop around them, Menuhkeu stopped. He pointed to eye-level markings in the bark of an oak, two crossed arrows. He ran his fingers over the hatching. "Weapemeok," he said. "They mark their oaks with this sign all through their territory."

Keeta's heart swelled. Her husband knew her so well, how she gathered information like others coveted polished shells. She enjoyed how he viewed her rising status as his strength, rather than a weakness. Keeta put her hand over her husband's, still resting on the tree trunk. The Roanoke didn't mark their trees. Their territory was islands and peninsula and needed no signs. "Where do I look to find these markings?" she asked.

"Look for the older trees and remember the ones you have seen. Most important is to recognize them when you come across them, so you know where you are."

In the fading light, they returned to camp. When Menuhkeu had told his father he wanted Keeta as a wife, his father had been unsure. Although her father, Adchaen, was a respected warrior, the family was small. Most of his relatives lived on Croatoan Island and his second wife, also from a small family, had only Keeta survive past birth. Wequassus, though, had heard of Keeta's skill in counting and encouraged the match for her son. Owush, whose wife was the most beautiful woman in Dasemunkepeuc, had been the most dismissive of his brother's choice. "Those herring clan people," Owush had scoffed, as many from the weasel clan did. "They can be slippery and unreliable, and sometimes need to be reminded of their duty."

It was Keeta's mind that moved as quickly as fish through the current, Menuhkeu should have answered, but Owush's influence often silenced Menuhkeu's tongue. Menuhkeu was proud of this quality in his wife, he should have answered. Now that others noticed and lauded her as well, Menuhkeu was content to say nothing and enjoy his good fortune.

Weapemeok and Choanoak Territory
The Trading Party Comes Choanoak Territory

The winter sun persisted in the cloudless sky. The small hunting party had returned two days ago with a large buck, and the group camped while they hung and dressed the carcass. The Roanoke would not hunt in Choanoak territory.

Sitting at the edge of the marsh, Keeta watched the water move from the distant sound. Gradually, as the tide turned to high, the slate-blue waves crept inland over the winter grass, reflecting the clear sky. Her growing baby fluttered inside her. As she sat, counts of beans and corn sorted through her mind. Keeta and First Mother had determined that this was a plenty-year, but how much would the mice eat from them over the winter? How accurate was the count on Roanoke or Croatoan Island? Would the wassadors, with Wanchese and Manteo, ever return?

When the incoming tide lapped at her feet, Keeta stood. All packed and ready to move again, it was time to pull out the canoes and journey onward.

By late afternoon the canoes had turned into the wide mouth of the Moratuk River. As they paddled upstream, the sun slipped below the approaching pines. Keeta watched shadows form along the strange bank. In the spring, when the water tumbled down from the mountains, these currents rushed and swirled, and travel upstream became more difficult. Now, farther from the sound, the water lost its brine, and ice congealed over depressions in the large boulders that rose over the waterline and limned the shallow inlets.

The canoes maneuvered between two icy boulders and pulled into an upstream pool. Menuhkeu used his paddle to crack the frozen surface. They had pulled into their last camp with noise and promises of a good deer, but now no one spoke, and they quickly tethered the canoes. Keeta gathered branches to make a shelter to serve all the travelers, who would camp close together tonight.

Making no fire, they ate the meat grilled yesterday. As the dark drew in Menuhkeu pulled Keeta aside, taking her hand. They walked a few feet into the underbrush. In the shadows, Keeta followed Menuhkeu's outstretched hand—carved into the wide oak in front of them was a circle the shape of the sun or the full moon, the sign of Choanoak territory.

During the night, clouds moved in from the west covering the stars, and the morning broke gray. The Roanoke quit camp quickly and, leaving their canoes, moved up the path toward Menatonon's village.

The trail cut through dense oak, pine, and bramble, and the low light lent a feeling of closeness unfamiliar to the Roanoke, who lived surrounded by water. Not too far along the path Pog, walking in front as scout, held up his hand and stopped. Three Choanoak appeared. Painted in their green and yellow in a pattern of broad stripes, they presented a fierce and unyielding group.

Wingina stepped up from the back. He reached slowly and deliberately into his quiver and took out a slender ash rod tied with crane feathers, into which four small arrows had been burnt—his greeting arrow.

He laid it flat across his palm and extended his arm.

A Choanoak came forward and lifted the arrow from Wingina's hand, nodding his acceptance. He spoke another's name. A very young warrior came forward, took the arrow, and retreated up the path.

In the silence that followed Keeta listened to the movement of the river in the distance. The rushing sound reminded her of the stories of the memegwasi, spirits that live in fresh, fast-moving waters and cause canoes to tip and people to drown. She wondered if such a big river would have more of these spirits, and how the Choanoak made peace with them.

Soon a large escort returned with the message that the Roanoke were welcome. By noon the Roanoke had settled into an area by the side of the river with the expectation that tomorrow they would meet with Menatonon.

Choanoak Territory
The Roanoke Meet with Menatonon and the Choanoak and the Weapemeoc

The Roanoke camped in a patch of red pines just outside the Choanoak village. With the men bathing in the river for the upcoming gathering, Keeta, already cleansed, rested by the low fire listening to the hum of activity from the nearby village. Menatonon had seven hundred warriors and this, his home, bustled. Children shouted to one another, their high voices carrying over the hum of activity. Fires crackled. Women laughed. Unused to being in a strange place, Keeta fingered the beads on her pouch, which reminded her of her parents. She touched the fish-rock, for strength. Taking a deep breath, she held her hands over the fire. Its warmth brought a centered feeling.

A cracking branch announced the approach of a young girl. Her long hair was gathered and tied back at her neck, not cut short in the front like the Roanoke girls. Along the side of her winter leggings, instead of a flat seam were small fringes with extra deerskin cut for decoration. Keeta found this innovation very pretty. The girl's expression mixed curiosity and some nervousness. "Hello, little sister," Keeta greeted her.

She smiled. "Come with me," she invited and beckoned with both hands.

Keeta stood and followed. As she went, her gaze turned. This village was much larger than any she had seen, with endless rows of lodges and countless people moving about. The path twisted through the busyness and Keeta worked hard to keep track of her steps so that she could find her way back, if necessary.

They entered a large lodge divided into many sections. Low flames flickered under three fire holes, spaced evenly along the roof mats. Like the Roanoke lodges, a long bench circled the interior, covered with bear and cougar skins along with the usual deer, squirrel, and rabbit. Keeta felt the weight of many eyes upon her and not one familiar face.

She felt alone. In all her fifteen years, she had never before sat down with people she did not know. Even those she met from Croatoan Island or elsewhere she had encountered when they visited Dasemunkepeuc, familiar ground, surrounded by familiar people. But the girl who had led her here smiled now, and two women came forward to take her hand, "Here is a soft seat," said one. Around her neck was a many-roped necklace of beads made of polished Roanoke shells. "And here is something to refresh you," said the other, who had inkings circling her hands. She handed Keeta a gourd of warm stew, the steam rising from the top.

"Thank you, aunts," replied Keeta. She took a taste. It was a familiar corn stew with venison and dried berries, her favorite. She smiled and thanked her hosts; she wasn't accustomed to eating berries in the winter. "I am Adtoekit," Keeta said, sharing her formal name and those around her smiled and told her their names as well.

Their talk began and Keeta followed it. She hadn't realized how close the Roanoke and Choanoak were in speech and manners. The woman with the beaded necklaces chatted comfortably. No one else in the lodge wore strung beads around her neck, but Keeta restrained from asking after the custom. "And how is Nootimis?" the woman asked, using First Mother's name. "We enjoy her company each winter." Yes, they all agreed, her company was a pleasure.

"She is well," answered Keeta, "and sends her greetings,"

although First Mother hadn't mentioned this group as she and Keeta had spent their time counting and analyzing. A small girl came over and laid her palms on Keeta's growing belly. An older woman passed her a baby to hold. His fat thighs reminded her of her new nephew Pishpesh.

The beaded woman took note of her pouch with its beads. "Such beautiful work the Roanoke do with the shells," she said. "There's nothing else like it." She paused slightly and Keeta thought suddenly of Wequassus, how easily she pulled information from people before they knew they had given anything up.

"Excuse me, but we are so curious." At this all other conversation in the lodge silenced.

Keeta smiled, half from nerves and half to stall time before she had to speak.

The beaded woman smiled back as if all she had to say were merely pleasantries. "Have you seen a wassador?"

Keeta knew that she should have expected this question. News traveled, and the wassadors had taken their small, odd canoes all around the sound for the short time their ships were in the bay. Maybe these Choanoak women had brought her here and fed her only to find out what she knew. "I haven't," she answered. From the beaded woman's reaction she understood that her answer was perceived as withholding and unfriendly. "I've only seen their ships," she added.

Any perception of rudeness dissipated in the buzz that followed. They didn't know the word, so Keeta explained. "Their canoes are very big, to carry them over the sea, and they call them ships. But they're too big for the sound, so they have little canoes as well." Keeta realized that many of these women had never seen the bay, so it would hard for them to understand how the ships nearly tipped over entering Roanoke fishing grounds. She was at an unfamiliar loss for words.

"We heard they were spirits from the other world," said the woman with the inkings on her wrists.

Keeta paused and wondered, how much should she share? How much of what she knew was tribal information? Yet here she was, the guest of a far more powerful tribe. She thought of Wequassus and tried to be as smooth and as pleasant. She thought of First Mother in order to remember to always protect her tribe.

"They appeared as men to us," she answered. "I was told by those who saw them that they were men."

"We heard as well that they have powerful, strange weapons and tools," the inked woman continued.

Keeta wondered if this were their First Mother, despite her lack of beads. She knew not to mention the sharp tool that had injured Peimacum, so she offered up something that seemed like special knowledge, yet also was instantly clear to all who met the visitors. "They wear metal clothing, a strange, hard metal."

Her audience considered this with some talk and speculation.

"So they aren't visitors from the spirit world?" the beaded woman asked.

Keeta considered this. "We don't know," she answered. "But they have white skin and are very hairy." This information set off another string of comments and conversations. "And they smell badly," she concluded. The children laughed at this and Keeta relaxed. She could go on about their stink for as long as she was a guest in the lodge. Menuhkeu had told her lots of stories.

The wind picked up from the west and slate-gray clouds moved across the sky. Wingina, Granganimeo, Aquandut, and Wampeikuc were absent, busy doing the bulk of the real negotiating before the big meeting. Menuhkeu returned from the river to find Keeta gone from their camp. He walked about the area, searching, until his brother took pity on him. "The women have taken her to visit in the main lodge, I am sure of it."

"He could have told you that earlier," commented Pog. "Before you followed every rustling squirrel looking for her."

Menuhkeu nodded. It was difficult enough to be in the Choanoak camp.

Pog echoed his thoughts. "They are so many."

Menuhkeu answered reflexively his father's oft-stated phrase, "Small in number is not weak," he said.

"And the big at heart are strong," finished Pog, who had grown up on Wampeikuc's teachings as well.

The Choanoak meeting ground was many times larger than the Roanoke council area, and throughout the afternoon many hundreds gathered around the large fire in the center. Flecks of snow fell.

When it was time, Menuhkeu strode in with his fellow warriors in their red and yellow and took his place with the Roanoke at the eastern side of the circle. Under the darkening sky, the tall pines at the edge of the meeting ground loomed larger, the meeting space shrinking under their guard. He was relieved when Keeta appeared shortly after and took her place between Wingina and Wampeikuc. Her full face and serious expression cheered Menuhkeu's heart. Granganimeo sat on Wingina's other side. Warriors in blue and yellow from Weapemeok and their weroance, Okisko, a solemn man, sat across from the Roanoke on the western side. The Choanoak warriors and advisors completed the circle.

When all were seated, the great Menatonon slowly crossed the grounds thronged with Choanoak villagers and their many visitors. A tall man with a narrow frame not unlike Wingina's, Menatonon stopped frequently to greet individuals before he reached the north end of the circle and sat. Copper bracelets lined both his arms. Snow gathered on the large-pawed cougar skin resting on his shoulders.

The Choanoak spirit traveler, single crow feather hanging down from his hair, chanted thank you to the Creator for the gathering of allies and friends, and the appowac pipe made its way around the broad circle.

With a nod from Menatonon, Wingina began the talking. In his sonorous voice, he spoke of how honored the Roanoke were to be so generously received by the great Choanoak. Menuhkeu understood that this tribute was expected—all the peoples in the tribute area would come and say similar honoring words. How else would Menatonon know who were his allies? Wingina praised Menatonon's wisdom and noted his trading routes in all directions, to the Mangoak of the Copper Mountains, and to the Powhatan of the north. Wingina reminded Menatonon that the Roanoke respected his keeping of the peace in the area, his keeping the trading routes open for all to prosper.

The great man, so old that the hair on his head had lines of white, nodded his appreciation.

After the tribute of words came the tribute of gifts, to strengthen the bonds between tribes. Aquandut stood. Menuhkeu was proud to have this tall, square-shouldered warrior bear the Roanoke offering. Carrying a deerskin pouch in his open palms, he strode purposefully across the circle to place the pouch at Menatonon's feet. At the weroance's nod, Aquandut opened the pouch to reveal a bounty of gleaming shells of purples and blues, polished into round beads. Wingina spoke then. He praised the goods the Roanoke had brought—the shining shells, the dried herring for the feast—and he boasted of the Roanoke's strengths. Menuhkeu was full of pride as Keeta nodded to Menatonon, to demonstrate that the Roanoke had prospered so well that they had fish to spare.

Menatonon bowed his head and took the pouch. These widely coveted shells, polished as only the Roanoke knew how, kept Menatonon's western alliances strong. This treasure would go on to be traded many times, gaining in value as it traveled farther and farther away from the beaches and from the people who made it.

Okisko of the Weapemeok tribe spoke next. Okisko was the youngest of the three weroances, not as smooth a talker as Wingina, but a strong man with a fierce reputation as a warrior. The Weapemeok boasted of almost three hundred warriors.

When the Weapemeok had given over their tribute, Menatonon turned to the Roanoke. "Now," he said. "Share with us what you know about the visitors."

A flurry of images came to Menuhkeu—the black dots riding on the sea, the metal-clad visitors nervously walking on the Roanoke Island beach, the metal tool wrapped in leather that Pog had taken from the ship. What of this would Wingina share?

Wingina spoke slowly and carefully. He described the wassadors' big canoes. He told of the two spirit travelers who had journeyed back over the sea with them. He described the wassadors' metal clothing, their white skin and hairy faces, their odd scent. Menuhkeu knew that much of these details had been told before, but speaking it aloud in the circle made the information shared knowledge, facts to come back to in the future.

Okisko asked about the size of their canoes. "He wants to know how easily they could travel up the bay to Weapemeok territory," Pog whispered to Menuhkeu.

Other Choanoak warriors asked about their weapons, the numbers of men, and their bravery.

"As many warriors as all of Weapemeok were on the two

canoes," answered Wampeikuc, ignoring the murmur of disbelief. "They carry wooden sticks that are noisemakers and have larger metal noisemakers on their ship. They also carry long metal weapons. As for their bravery, we did not test it."

Some of the warriors around the circle exchanged knowing looks, as if to say, of course not, you are the Roanoke. Menuhkeu burned with anger. Let's see what you would have done, he wanted to answer, but didn't. Angry words are arrows, his father had often said. Send them with care.

"We heard that the Secotan weroance of Pomeioc was injured by a visitor's weapon," said Okisko. The Weapemeok warriors listened with keen attention. "That he received a deep wound from a single blow."

"The visitors wouldn't trade their weapons with us," replied Wampeikuc.

"Such a weapon would be very valuable," said Menatonon, who had said little since he had received his tributes. "It would give great benefit to those small in numbers."

"It would also be a great gift," answered Wingina as the snow fell more thickly. "If they return, as they say they will, we will bring one to you at next year's council."

The Choanoak nodded their approval.

Menuhkeu regarded Wingina with respect. His weroance had been promising the sky to the moon for many seasons, and no one had yet come to collect it.

The talk broke after Wingina's promise. Snow fell more quickly, covering the village in white. Choanoak women moved in from all sides with steaming pots of stew for the many guests. Menuhkeu felt the bounty of the occasion, perhaps more so, he realized, since meeting the wassadors. Before his visit to the ship, the young warrior had never considered that hosts could reflect want rather than plenty.

As Wampeikuc noted on the trip home, the balance was kept for now. The Roanoke went home with armbands of copper and protection from the north and west in exchange for polished shells, dried fish and the willingness to remain between the populated inlands and the unknown sea.

Dasemunkepeuc
Keeta Gives Birth to Mishontoowau

From the Creator comes the slanting light, slicing through
bare trees in the spring and fall, warming the earth. From
the Creator comes the sky, and all creatures live under its
protection. This Keeta knew in her heart. From the time she
was carried on her mother's back, chewing on her Mama's
hair for comfort and pleasure, she has known this.

When Keeta's belly grew round and hard, she felt the
Creator's energy in her like a ray of sun, warming and nour-
ishing, as the baby grew and made itself known. As the full
moon of coming fish made its way across the night sky just
before the herring returned, the baby determined to leave
the spirit world and enter the human realm.

Keeta's belly tightened and loosened, tightened and loosened, while the life within her shifted, searching for the path
out. When her breath grew short and the squeezing pulled
so deeply that Keeta went in and out of awareness—a switch
as abrupt as sleep to wakefulness—Keeta knew it was time
to fetch her Mama. She squeezed Menuhkeu's hand; he had
lain awake listening to his wife's labored breath for most of
the long night. Laying her palm on his chest to keep him
in bed, Keeta rolled out of their blanket. She picked up the
pile of mats she had prepared over the past months and left
the lodge. Deep in the evening, the large white moon glim-
mered from the west. She stopped when her belly tightened
and moved when it loosened, and the chill felt good against
her sweating skin.

Keeta knocked lightly at the lodge entrance and Mama

was at the door, almost before Keeta's hand lowered. Mama took the mats, and together they made their way toward the stream. Along the way Mama fetched Naana for the medicine to ease the birth.

Now the tightening came closer and closer together, lengthening the short walk. By the running water, Mama lay the mats down on a soft, mossy area.

Keeta closed her eyes, glad to have her Mama and Naana nearby. Her wet skin prickled at the cold in the earth. The whoosh of the racing spring stream echoed the whoosh of blood running inside her, and she relaxed into it. Her body worked apart from her thoughts and she let it—to fight her clenching belly would be to fight the spirit trying to enter the world.

Mama and Naana covered Keeta with moss and mats to stop her heat from leaving. While Naana readied the medicine over a small fire, Mama massaged her daughter's hands and feet and softly sang the story of the people's beginning. As she sang, Keeta felt something pent up inside her freeing itself, like a fish carried down a rushing stream.

Mama sang of Nanabohzo hunting. "With racing steps he chased a deer who dove into the middle of a vast lake. He chased a bear who dove into the same lake. Then he chased a cougar. Then a raccoon. Nanabohzo," Mama chanted, "Nanabohzo dove into the water after them, following all the creatures who fell through a great hole in the middle of the waters, an opening into which fell all of the world."

Naana knelt next to Keeta. "Take this," she whispered. She held Keeta's head in one hand and brought a tea of barks and herbs to her lips with the other so that Keeta could drink the medicine Wautog prepared for women to release their babies. The drink was unfamiliar, dank and hard to swallow, so Keeta took it in small sips, Naana encouraging her with nods.

Mama continued. "The world now covered in water, where would the creatures settle? Nanabohzo sent out crow. Crow searched in the direction of the four winds, but he found nothing but water as far as he could fly."

Keeta felt a rush of warm water spread out of her. Naana patted her arm, "That was good," she encouraged.

Then Keeta felt as if the ground below her back disappeared, as well as the moonlight and the sound of the river. Lost to herself, she was aware only of an intense pulling across her hips, a power greater than she. She fought off exhaustion and brought her mind to her belly to move with the waves of tightening.

"Nanabohzo, Nanabohzo, what will you do now, with no land?" asked Mama, her voice rising. "Send out otter to search. Nanabohzo waited many days, but otter returned half-drowned."

Keeta sat up, Mama holding her shoulders, Naana at her feet.

"Nanabohzo, is all lost for the creatures of the world? But then muskrat said, I will go. I will find land. Muskrat dove down, deeper and deeper into the water. Muskrat was gone many days. Nanabohzo had just about given up hope, when muskrat poked her head out of the water."

The waves of power rushed toward Keeta's hips and she followed them, pushing along at each wave.

"Muskrat held out a paw-full of earth. Nanabohzo took the earth and put it on turtle's back, and there all the creatures gathered to live. Nanabohzo married muskrat and together they created the first people, from which we come."

Keeta felt a release and then she heard it—the birth cry.

"A boy!" cried out Naana. "A boy!"

Intensity gone, Keeta felt instantly slack and worn. She craned forward to see. Naana handed her the cord. "Bite down hard," said Mama. "Release him."

Keeta bent over the slippery cord, put it between her teeth and bit quickly. As she did she felt her baby's spirit leave her like a puff of wind, to go his own way. She received the wisdom that this was the first of many leavings that each life contains. She also felt that her life as a girl had also gone like a puff of smoke. Her body ached as it returned to her.

The boy responded with a cry and a protest. Naana handed the wet, squirming body to Keeta and the new mother pulled the child to her warmth. She put her lips to his hands, his fingers, his feet, his toes, and his round head covered in wet fur, like a muskrat. She did this quickly for the air was cold. They would take him home and bathe him in warm water by the fire. For now, though, Keeta wrapped the boy in a raccoon pelt, the soft fur against his new skin. She put moss between his legs to catch what he would soon expel, the last remains of his life underwater.

And they named him Mishontoowau, the boy who makes himself heard.

A Wassador Feast

Dasemunkepeuc
The Wassadors Return

Menuhkeu strode through the ancestor trees, a large net balanced on his shoulders. A soft blanket of fragrant cedar leaves muffled his steps. Soon the bluefish would be running, and the net he carried was strong enough to resist the fish's sharp teeth, a predator that raced and leapt through the water's surface in frenzied schools after smaller prey.

As an occasional wave broke on the beach, its distant echoes reaching inland, as if carried on the grove's deep shadow. The summer breeze also carried the calls of small children playing a popular hunting game—a dove coo here, a snarling panther there, cries of surprise, trills of laughter. Menuhkeu listened with attention. His Mishoo would be playing the same kinds of games in a few seasons. Throughout Menuhkeu's childhood, every day had presented his father an opportunity to teach and Menuhkeu to learn. Drifting asleep in their lodge, the family had played I know what owl speaks. As a baby running and falling in the beach sand, Wampeikuc distracted Menuhkeu with two pieces of rope and a lesson on knots. Menuhkeu still remembered Owush grabbing the strings, tying them deftly together, and tossing the knot back into his lap. He smiled to think of how angry he had been at his more adept brother, and yet how that humiliation had pushed him to keep up.

As if summoned, Owush appeared in the distance, racing along the path. Even in the half-light, Menuhkeu saw how Owush's square jaw and broad shoulders looked more and more like their father's as he aged.

"What's the hurry," Menuhkeu began, stopping to meet his brother. Owush interrupted him with a shake of his head.

"A Croatoan scout just brought news."

Menuhkeu's chest tightened with worry.

"Seven ships this time," said Owush, using the wassador term they had all adopted for large canoes. "Some already within our sight, to the south of us." The brothers looked at each other. Menuhkeu felt at once as if everything he had ever understood and cared about was about to be scattered in a big wind. Even if he had known how to put this fear into words, he wouldn't have shared this with his level-headed, practical brother.

He shifted his shoulder toward the beach. "The nets?"

Owush shrugged. "We still have to eat."

Hidden in the pines behind the sands, the Roanoke watched from the shore. As in the season before, the ships didn't turn easily from the rough sea into the calm bay—the spot where the water leaving fought the water coming. The sky hung blue, but in the narrow straight the gray waves shifted, moving and angry. Clearly Mishibijiw the water panther prowled underneath the surface. The panther tossed up wave after wave, tipping their ships from side to side. In response, the wassadors scrambled up and down their posts, pulling at ropes, angling the white mats.

One ship after another, tipping and rocking, lurched from the sea through the gap. Mishibijiw turned angrier. He tossed the waves higher, forcing the fourth ship a little closer to the shore. This one tilted more deeply than the others. Once the water panther found a weak spot, he did not give up. The wassadors worked the ropes quickly, climbing up and down the posts like squirrels.

The water panther pressed harder. As the waves crested high over the sides of the ship, the posts tipped to the side, lower and lower. When the ship lingered on its side for a second too long, Mishibijiw pounced—he sent a huge, drowning wave into the boat. The ship fell at once on its side, water poured in, and soon it lay stuck in the sand.

By now the panther was tired. Three more ships rocked and tossed but made their way into the bay. One panther, seven ships, a tough fight.

Keeta wiped the milk dribbling out of Mishoo's mouth just before the white trickled over his chin and down his neck. The evening remained as hot and muggy as the day and most of Dasemunkepeuc was still awake, outside of the stuffy lodges, catching what breeze they could. All around her, Keeta saw the lights of other fires throughout the village, flickering like fireflies in the dark.

Nearby Pishpesh lay asleep. Minneash idly pushed her son's chubby foot back on the deerskin when he kicked it off, while Mama and Wequassus sang in low voices.

Menuhkeu arrived back from Wingina's council and settled in next to Keeta. Pensive and quiet, Keeta turned to him with a questioning look, but the quick arrival of the others—Wampeikuc, Owush, and her father, Adchaen—stopped any response.

The warriors sat. They refused Wequassus's offer of stew and continued a conversation that had begun much earlier.

"No sign of Wanchese?" Keeta quietly asked her husband.

Menuhkeu shook his head. "Or Manteo," he added, anticipating his wife's next question.

Adchaen looked to his daughter. "No news of Wanchese, but we have news that Manteo has been traveling with the wassadors while they visit other villages."

The women stayed quiet, so Keeta asked the question that was on their minds. "What other villages?"

"Secotan, Pomeioc..." said Menuhkeu.

At the mention of the enemy village, Owush snorted.

"Why would they visit our enemies?" asked Keeta.

Owush shook his head.

"Aquascognok…"

"That's a Weapemeok village!" interrupted Keeta.

"Not anymore," said Wampeikuc grimly.

"The wassadors burnt it down," explained Menuhkeu at last.

"They burnt all the lodges and all their fields," added Owush.

"What?" exclaimed Wequassus. "Did the fire burn out of control?"

"We hear they burnt the fields first," said Wampeikuc.

Wampeikuc and Adchaen exchanged glances. "We hear that the wassadors lost an object of much value, a gourd," explained Wampeikuc. "A metal gourd," he added in response to the confused faces. "A metal gourd from their own village. They said the Weapemeok took the gourd from them, unfairly."

Keeta felt cold all at once—you do not burn your enemies' lodges without first asking them to give you payment for your harm and if no payment is given, you raid the village and the fields before you burn them down. It was inconceivable that anyone would burn food. These actions struck Keeta as more like a storm or a drought rather than the behavior of a person. The silence grew. "Did they say why?" Keeta asked at last.

"It seems they value metal above all else," concluded Adchaen as he rose to leave.

Mishoo cried out in his sleep. Keeta thought of the tool Pog had taken from the wassador's ship. Would they lose their fields as well?

Mama rose too and took her leave, but only after touching her daughter and grandson softly on the cheek.

Dasemunkepeuc
Wanchese the Spirit Traveler Returns

The rising sun grayed the black sky as Wanchese stood on the wet deck of the wassador ship. Land appeared on the horizon as distant smoke. With wide smiles and cold eyes the wassadors had told him he was going home, but only when the fog cleared to reveal a familiar stretch of sand and pines did the spirit traveler believe them.

The green sight of the approaching shore, the same one he had watched slowly disappearing four seasons ago, delivered a rush of pleasure so intense that Wanchese exhaled aloud. He fully felt, then, the length of his time away.

Later, after the ship had fought its battle to enter the calm bay, Wanchese fought himself to betray nothing as he sat in the smaller canoe, which was lowered off the side of the ship and into the water.

As the boat paddled forward, the shore grew larger. Wanchese took in the pleasant scent of warm sand. He discerned the gently shifting grasses, the reddish blanket of needles under the pines, and a great heron that rose, broad winged, on a current of air. He recognized that they were far south of Roanoke territory, south even of Secotan territory.

The canoe thudded into the shallows. In the shifting of the sails and the maneuvering of the craft over the breaking waves, Wanchese slipped out of the vessel.

The water dropped from his chest to his knees to his feet and then he was on the familiar sand, the heat of it rising up like an embrace.

Shouting followed him but he continued forward through

the nicking grasses, into the quiet pines. Wanchese knew the wassadors wouldn't follow. They were too afraid.

When he had put some distance between them, he tore off their clothes—the close-fitting top and overlying vest, the shoes on his feet, the trousers on his legs.

Now naked, the wind flowing through the pines cleared his thoughts. The cry of a gray gull overhead felt as if it came directly from his own mouth, as he headed north, toward Dasemunkepeuc. Long into the future, as Wanchese lay dying, this freeing moment would return to him as the blessing of the Creator come to take him home.

Dasemunkepeuc
Manteo Returns

Sightings of Manteo, in Secotan, on the Albemarle Sound, arrived before the spirit traveler returned to Dasemunkepeuc in person, riding in the back of a wassador canoe in the same straight-backed manner in which he had left, four seasons ago.

Slicing their long, narrow paddles through the water, the wassadors made their way to the shore of Dasemunkepeuc. They deposited the spirit traveler on the beach and paddled back to one of their ships.

Asku greeted Manteo as he stepped into the pines and out of view from the retreating wassador canoe. He would later tell Menuhkeu how strange it was to see Manteo wearing wassador clothes; a soft shirt grasped his neck and wrists, breeches covered his legs, and hard moccasins protected his feet, despite the warm weather. Only once Asku noticed the spirit traveler's black crow feather behind his ear was the young warrior convinced that the person standing there really was Manteo and not a confused vision, something rising in the heatwaves off the sand.

Asku signaled with a whistle that a friend approached. The news of Manteo's return swept through the village. Work ceased as the people joined to welcome him back and also to question him about the many ships in the harbor, and ask for news of Wanchese.

At the meeting grounds, Chepeck lit appowac to ease the traveler's return, and the people crowded around the council circle to hear Wingina's welcome. "How glad we are you have returned," welcomed Wingina, his tone warm.

As the crowd continued to gather, lines of thin, white clouds and wind from the west blew in, bringing some relief from the muggy heat. Menuhkeu, sitting with Asku and Pog, looked over the Roanoke faces, all turned to Manteo, waiting for what he had to share. Manteo, who had always enjoyed attention, seemed now to be unaware of the eyes upon him. The young spirit traveler took many deep breaths of the appowac. He closed his eyes and bowed his head for some long minutes.

"Twelve kizis I have been gone from you," he began formally, as if delivering a rehearsed message. "During that time, I have learned the wassador language and many of their customs and habits. I have met their weroance, the white-faced woman. I taught their spirit traveler our words."

Menuhkeu and Asku exchanged glances. A tribe's language is meant for the tribe's benefit and is something that can only be given, not taken. The Roanoke language was understandable only to Roanoke allies. The powerful Mangoak to the west didn't share their language with their enemies; only select Choanoak people learned it for trade, and it would not occur to anyone else to bother. Had Manteo joined another tribe? What had he done in order to learn wassador words?

At this, people parted for Wanchese's wife, Wunne Wadsh, running in from her fields. She stood at the edge of the council circle sweaty and out of breath, her thick hair askew. "And my husband?" she asked. "What do you know?"

"Wanchese left his hosts just after we arrived and hasn't been heard from since," answered Manteo. He watched Wunne Wadsh carefully. "I thought you might know where he is."

A cloud passed over her face; she took back the next question on her lips and turned away.

Pog leaned over toward Menuhkeu. "Where's Manteo's

cougar skin?" he whispered. "He left wearing his cougar skin."

Manteo continued in a raised voice. "The wassadors have returned to trade and to learn our ways." He met the faces of his people gathered around the circle, listening and watching. "They have much to teach us. And...they want to visit for a longer while."

The west wind increased. Dirt tossed up, and large, white clouds scudded across the sky.

Menuhkeu thought of the sharp tool Pog had taken, how useful it was, how good it would to have many more of them.

"Why have they brought seven ships?" asked Wingina, addressing both Manteo and the people.

"Their large numbers and great strength are beyond our counting. But only some of them want to stay here for longer," Manteo answered, his voice even, as if he were relaying information well known and previously discussed.

"Did they bring any women?" asked the elderly Ensenore. "Do they have any women? Or children?"

"They have women," Manteo assured them. "But," he hesitated. "There aren't any on the ships."

"Is it true," continued Wingina, his voice firm, his long body projecting command, "that the wassadors have been north?"

The people grew quiet. Scouts had been delivering rumors of the various places the wassadors had been for almost a week, visiting villages all around the Roanoke territory.

Manteo nodded.

"And they skirmished with the Weapemeok, killing twenty or more of their warriors and taking some of their women?" People visibly shifted uncomfortably. This and the story of the burned fields had been the only talk for weeks.

"I did not know this," answered Manteo, looking quickly from side to side. "But they want to meet with you and your cousin," he added, indicating Wingina and Granganimeo.

"They request a council."

Wingina nodded, and Wampeikuc leaned in and whispered something to the weroance. "We will discuss this," said Wampeikuc.

Manteo understood that they would discuss this without him. He stood. He would not stay the night at Dasemunkepeuc, he explained. He would leave with the wassadors and then travel to Croatoan to see his weroance mother and the others of his family. He would return in a few days to hear the tribe's response to the wassador request.

Menuhkeu, Asku, and Pog lingered together before heading home, Menuhkeu to the new lodge he shared with Keeta and Mishoo; Asku and Pog, each without partners, to their family lodges.

"So Wanchese is back?" questioned Menuhkeu.

"Yes, but no one knows where he is," replied Asku.

"This doesn't feel right," said Pog.

"Wingina has been balancing our friends and enemies for a long time," answered Asku. "We have no reason to distrust Manteo."

"Where's his cougar skin?" insisted Pog. "Did he trade it to learn their words?"

"He's a spirit traveler," countered Menuhkeu. "He needed to learn their words."

"Did he have to tell them ours?" asked Pog. "And why is he wearing their clothes?"

"What would you have us do?" questioned Asku. "Clearly we have no choice but to meet with them."

"Do you think Ensenore's looking for a wassador wife?" joked Menuhkeu, breaking the uneasy silence. "He won't stop asking about the wassador women."

The three burst into laughter. "It would be his fourth," noted Asku.

"Saving the best for last," added Pog.

At the sound of approaching footsteps, the three grew quiet.

Manteo approached, slowing his stride as if to stop and have a word.

"Welcome home," said Pog.

"Yes," agreed Menuhkeu and Asku. "We're glad you're back."

"Thank you," answered Manteo.

Pog broke the ensuing silence. "Have a safe journey back to Croatoan."

Manteo nodded his thanks, picked up his pace, and continued along.

As he slipped into the growing darkness, Menuhkeu regretted their coldness toward someone their own age, someone who had shared their moon trek. But the damage having already been done, the four headed their separate ways.

Dasemunkepeuc
Adchaen Ahtuck Bathes his Grandson

The wassador ships sat in the harbor.

But still the corn had to be ground and the berries picked. The west wind sent quick clouds in across the sky. Leaves rustled their gentle summer song.

Today Wequassus planned to heat her quartz stone and maintain an even fire for making bread, corn bread with summer berries.

"Listen, Mishoo," Keeta said to her son who was strapped into his cradle on her back. "We're going to have something wonderful to eat."

As Keeta ground the corn, Mishoo wriggled on her back. "Watch the kernels get smaller and smaller," she chanted. "Smaller and smaller."

She stopped mid-voice and looked up. Adchaen stood waiting for his daughter to take notice of him. Before she could stand straight, he came to her and touched her hair as if she were still a child. Untying the straps, for Mishoo was securely fastened in for a day of work, Adchaen lifted the baby from his cradle. Mishoo laughed when he was freed and made a grab for his grandfather's nose. The warrior held him up high and took a few turns of flying him like a bird before he took him firmly in his arms and turned and left with him. Keeta followed.

They walked swiftly toward the river. Once at the river, Adchaen removed the tied moss that was Mishoo's diaper and clasped his hands around the baby's chest. Mishoo's head was firm on his neck, and small rolls of fat circled his legs. Keeta was proud of his sturdy little body, square and meaty, built like his father.

Adchaen stepped into the water until he was waist high. The current raced around him, moving over the rocky bottom toward the sea. He raised the baby high in the air and lowered him into the rushing water until he was completely covered. Mishoo emerged coughing and startled. Adchaen dipped him in two more times. Mishoo of the loud voice said nothing.

Mishoo's skin was mottled with small bumps from the chill of the water; even in the summer the water ran cool as it came from the mountains.

"Every morning, he must be dipped. He must be hardy," Keeta's father said as he handed his grandson back to her. "There are ships in the harbor," he admonished her.

Keeta pulled her baby close. She kissed his wet hair and smoothed it down with her fingers as he reached for the milk that had produced his sweet rolls of fat.

Dasemunkepeuc
Wunne Wadsh Tells of Wanchese's Return

Wunne Wadsh interrupted her story to smile to herself
every now and then, a break in her narrative of Wanchese's
return to Dasemunkepeuc. This irritated some of her listeners, but it was a diversion Keeta found charming, evidence
of the older woman's affection for her husband.

Wequassus had invited Wanchese's only wife to help prepare the food—the bluefish stew, smoked oysters, sassafras
water, and corn bread—for the wassador visit. With little
prompting Wunne Wadsh agreed, for Wequassus had shown
her many kindnesses over the preceding year.

"As soon as the ships were spotted coming up the coast, I
cooked a stew of blackberries, beans, and squash, along with
some plants," Wunne Wadsh related as she stood grinding
corn.

"What sort of plants?" asked Keeta, who wondered what
plants would help ease the transition from one world to
the next.

Keeta's mother-in-law's nostrils flared, which meant she regarded that detail as unimportant. "They were from Wautog,"
Wunne Wadsh answered. "I put them all in a pot, a pot
marked with healing pictures of my clan."

These healing pictures Keeta knew well—fish and water
images were the most powerful.

"My family," and here Wunne Wadsh smiled to herself
again. The small group gathered to help cook, Wequassus,
Minneash, Mama, and Keeta, knew who she meant. Her
son, a young warrior, and her oldest girl and her husband

and baby all had lived in the lodge with Wunne Wadsh and Wanchese before the spirit traveler had left. "When they saw me place the stew snug in the ashes by the fire, they hoped that their father was close by and would come home soon."

Although Roanoke women wore their hair short in the front, Wunne Wadsh's fell forward as she looked down at her work. She pushed a stray strand behind her ear in a precise way that Keeta recognized, this woman with gray in her hair and a body that showed the signs of hard work still longed for her husband. Keeta felt a pang of sadness at the year Wunne Wadsh had just endured. Heat washed over Keeta's face, and she chastised herself for only now understanding why Wequassus had so often walked by the other woman's lodge, "just to give greetings to Wunne Wadsh."

"The day had been so hot, you remember, and I opened all the roof flaps to the hazy half-moon, even after the bats had come out and the cicadas sang their evening song." Wunne Wadsh was now lost in her own story.

"When the insects and the village quieted and the moon set, I awoke to find Wanchese sleeping next to me. I was so afraid I was dreaming, I didn't move, in case even a twitch would break this vision, my happiness." She hesitated here. "So I dropped back to sleep." At this, even Wequassus took a moment to reflect on the scene.

"Then in the morning, the sun streaming in, I was alone. Usually the first up, I worried over my long sleep and my dream—had Wanchese's spirit come to say good-bye before it left for the place from which there is no easy return? With this in mind, I stepped outside to tend to the fire and begin my work for the day." At this point in the story, her small smiles changed into a broad grin.

"And there by the fire sat my Wanchese, our youngest son so close to his father, the others gathered around him. 'Mama Wunne,' my husband called to me, 'did you enjoy your sleep?'"

Murmurs of appreciation for the story came from every listener.

"My husband," she continued in a quieter voice, although no one had asked, "he is the same and not the same. But his joy of return is real, and that's what we claim for ourselves, when the memories of where he has been darken his spirit."

Wondering precisely what had darkened Wanchese's spirit worried Keeta, but it was hard for her to imagine, for Wanchese was a person who had always struck Keeta as somewhat mysterious.

Wunne Wadsh poured the corn she had ground into a gourd, knocking carefully at the sides of the pestle to gather every bit. "And later in the morning Wingina himself came by. He sat with us, drinking sassafras tea. And..." Here her voice quieted even more. "He held Wanchese like a son, close to his chest, head in his hands."

The listeners were touched into further silence. "Yes, Wingina is father to us all," said Wequassus finally.

Dasemunkepeuc
Wassadors Visit Dasemunkepeuc and Wequassus Serves a Feast

The day of the wassador visit was hot and still. Flat, gray
clouds pressed down from the sky.

Keeta and Minneash carried a large pot of bluefish stew
to the cooking fire, set up just outside the meeting circle.
The oily fish left a tasty surface layer of congealed fat, which
would melt into the rest of the stew when reheated.

Wequassus selected a small group of women and girls who
could be counted on to serve the food with grace and without
foolishness. "It's a shame your lovely friend Auwepu married into the shell polishers on Roanoke Island," Wequassus
complained to Keeta more than once. "She would have been
the perfect person to serve the first bowl."

Unconcerned that Wequassus had judged Keeta unfit to
serve food, Mishoo still in his cradle on her back, Keeta
itched to be near First Mother, sitting near Wingina at the
council circle.

As the morning progressed, hangers-on lingered at the food
area. Wequassus made an attempt to shoo them away, but
to no avail. In the growing anticipation, only the oldest and
most routine-bound people were absent. By the time the sun
hit the middle of the sky, most of the village had gathered
around in the meeting circle, waiting for the wassadors.
While many of those on Roanoke Island had seen the wassadors on their last visit, only a few from Dasemunkepeuc,
and these all warriors, had seen them up close. Wanchese's
quiet return without yet speaking publicly about his experience and the sight of Manteo's new clothes added to the

mystery and the tension.

Then came the news: the wassadors had landed on the beach and twelve of them would visit. The chattering around Keeta quieted. In the windless day the silence felt heavy and slow. After what felt like a very long time, Keeta spotted Granganimeo leading the group in. The Roanoke Island weroance wore ropes of pearl from his ears, copper bracelets on his arms. Then came Manteo, in his soft clothes and shoes.

Naana appeared at her side. "Where have you been?" whispered Keeta.

Naana shook her head. "Wautog! It's the new moon and she had so many plants to gather!"

Then Keeta saw them, her first glimpse. It was so strange. Despite the summer heat they were covered in a dull metal from head to toe, only their white faces visible. Fearsome suits, like that of an armadillo. One had an unfamiliar red feather coming out of his hat, was he the weroance?

Also strange was the silence. No one spoke, either to whisper to a neighbor or to call out a greeting. Even Mishoo was still.

The remaining metal-dressed ones emerged from the trees, with Roanoke warriors at points on every side. Keeta saw Asku standing near the meeting circle, and then Menuhkeu, behind the group and to the left. As they approached, she heard Manteo talking in strange words and pointing to the circle. Naana looked at Keeta, her eyes wide. "He understands them!"

When the group had gathered, Wingina emerged from the lodges and sat at the meeting circle. Wingina also wore his copper bracelets, his pearls, and his bearskin. Chepeck, in his rabbit cloak, strode over, joining the circle as he sat down to Wingina's right. Along came First Mother wearing her pearls. She took her place next to Chepeck. Wampeikuc, who had walked up from the beach with the escort, sat as always to Wingina's left. Granganimeo and Ensenore arranged themselves next. Manteo sat next to the one with the red feather in his hat, and eight of the wassadors settled themselves opposite. Four remained standing. Keeta wondered at their strategy. Roanoke warriors, including her father and Menuhkeu, stood guard all along the village. These visitors were here only as their guests. But surely they knew that.

Wingina brought out his long pipe, made of red clay from the spirit grounds far away, traded for through the Choanoak. Deer sinew twisted in a swirled pattern around the bowl, and crane feathers, in honor of his bird clan, hung from its stem. He lit and drew, and he passed it to Chepeck. Granganimeo, speaking quietly, drew attention to the three wassadors he recognized from the year before—a yellow-haired one called Barlowe, a sharp-chinned man with watery eyes called Harriot, and a wide-shouldered man called White, who carried a large bag. Keeta, standing with Naana and the rest of the village behind the council circle, attempted to identify the strange faces. One indeed had yellow hair on his face, and another a small, pointed chin. She could only guess at which of the others was this White, for they all possessed broad shoulders.

Manteo indicated the man with the feather, and Granganimeo passed the smoking bowl to him. Then back and forth the pipe went, until all seated had smoked.

Wequassus quit the crowd to check on her stew but Keeta remained. She studied the red-feathered man's face, as unmoving as a stone on the beach, as well as the man seated to his right. Short-legged but thick, with black hair on his face, his lips curled inward before he put the pipe to them. When he breathed in, his face indicated no pleasure, even something closer to distaste. Some of the other wassadors smiled and nodded and seemed to enjoy the pipe very much, perhaps happy of the way the appowac worked so quickly to sharpen the mind and set the blood flowing.

When the one with the feather spoke, Manteo translated. "This is their weroance, Grenville," he said. "He sends his greetings and thanks you for this meeting."

Wingina returned the greetings. As was proper, he recounted last year's visit and the friendship formed between them. He said he hoped the friendship could continue. He made no mention of the various other visits the wassador had made to the area in the interim.

"Harriot of the sharp chin watches our lips as we speak," whispered Naana. Keeta took a deep breath to dispel her feeling of unease at this revelation.

Minneash appeared at their side. "Wequassus says it's time to serve the stew."

"I thought she said she didn't need us for that," said Keeta, lifting her shoulders up and down and giving Mishoo a little ride. Naana, smiling, reached up and played with the baby's fingers.

"The girls are a little nervous. No one wants to go first," answered Minneash.

Back at the stew fire, Wequassus had solved the dilemma. When she, a mother four times over and a grandmother as well, had looked over the girls' frozen faces and felt their nerves, she had laughed. "What good are you young girls when it's the old lady who has to serve!" Taking a bowl she stood straight, her pearls dangling at her shoulders. She served the strangers as respected friends, indicating only welcome. The girls copied Wequassus's manner. This courtesy made little difference though, for the wassadors took no notice of the servers as they circled around with the food. They merely reached up and took the offering, without a glance at the server. None responded with the customary thankfulness, save the pointed-chin man, Harriot, who said something unintelligible to the young girl who served him, causing her to almost lose her composure and giggle.

Keeta left the spooning out to Minneash and stepped closer to the circle. Learning and watching made her less nervous. Her eyes returned to the one with black hair on his face, the one who had frowned at the pipe. A long metal tool and a carved wooden stick at his side, he appeared uncomfortable as he sat, twisting and untwisting his legs.

Shortly another problem beset Wequassus, as one wassador held up his empty bowl. She glanced at Manteo for help in understanding what the wassador meant. "He would like some more," Manteo said. She gave him a look, really? Manteo nodded, yes. Thinking he must be especially hungry, Wequassus took his bowl and refilled it. Then, one by one, the wassadors requested more. The stew disappeared from the pot. Still they wanted more. A veteran of many feasts, Wequassus had never before fed such hungry guests. She sent for some pemmican and dried fish from her stores and they ate that as well. When they began to request even more, she pretended not to understand, thinking it must be some kind of trick, to eat so much in one sitting.

The one called Harriot again spoke some of what may have been Roanoke words, but his meaning remained unclear.

"Don't worry," Manteo assured Wingina, as he turned and acknowledged Harriot with a smile. "He is very bad with our words and won't understand anything you say." Harriot smiled back and nodded his head. But still Harriot repeated himself and this time his words were more recognizable. "Wanchese," he said. He was asking about Wanchese. No one answered. Keeta felt as if her thoughts had been invaded, having this strange person mouth the familiar name.

Manteo busied himself with his stew, but Harriot was persistent and repeated Wanchese's name several times. Their weroance took notice; Grenville called out, "Manteo!"

This direct address turned all eyes on Manteo, for this

was not how the Roanoke addressed each other, chasing after speech when one has chosen to ignore another's words. Manteo answered him in their language, his calm face revealing nothing. While Grenville's face remained stony, Harriot seemed disappointed in Manteo's answer. Keeta sensed that Manteo didn't betray his companion.

After the meal was finished, Manteo announced that the wassadors had gifts. Yellow-haired Barlowe strode back to the beach. The Roanoke audience relaxed a bit at this news. Visitors who brought gifts, this was familiar behavior, and curiosity as to what the gift might be loosened some tongues. A sharp noise cracked the air, stopping conversation. Some of the children cried out.

"It's only a signal," said Manteo quickly. "Barlowe set off his weapon as a signal to the big ship."

While not comforted by this information, the audience waited quietly for what would come next. Wingina spoke a few words with Wampeikuc.

A short while later, Barlowe emerged from the cedars leading three women toward the edge of the meeting circle. From their hair, short on the sides and long on the back, the fringe on their skirts and the manner of their tattoos, they were Weapemeok.

Keeta couldn't breathe. How had this happened? How had the wassadors managed to capture these women? The Weapemeok had five times as many warriors as the Roanoke.

Body to body, the women stood close together. Visible dirt on their legs and hands, they hadn't bathed recently. One appeared pregnant and another had a streak of blood running along her calf. They looked down at the ground, their faces blank. The one with child looked at the fire and the pot of stew and a flash of emotion crossed her face before she looked back down at her feet.

Barlowe exclaimed something in his own words, his manner proud. Manteo translated, a gift.

Eyes turned to Wingina, who signaled his acceptance with a quick rotation of his palm. Grenville smiled and the wassadors copied his pleased expressions.

Mama stepped forward and pulled on Keeta's arm. "Come," she whispered. Keeta knew at once what her mother was up to, and together they approached the group of women. Naana and Minneash quickly followed. They led the women away from the circle. Despite the heat, Keeta felt their cold hands, their dry skin. They needed to drink. In hushed, soothing tones Mama welcomed them, took their hands one by one, rubbing them between her own. She reminded them of the custom of all the people—that now they were part of the Roanoke family and they would be cared for as such. One by one the women lifted their eyes to Mama's face and embraced her. At her command, the rest of the Roanoke women walked forward and led these new members away, so that they could bathe and be fed and find their new homes, their new families.

Meanwhile, the weroance Grenville at last spoke his mind. A group of the wassadors would stay with the Roanoke on their territory, and visit a while.

After the wassadors retreated to their ships, the council met. After the council dispersed, Keeta walked quickly under the starless sky.

She found Naana outside her lodge, heating some tea for her ailing mother. Naana didn't seemed surprised at the late visit, but this was Naana after all, a fern had probably alerted her, laughed Keeta to herself, partly in order to leaven her own dark mood. She sat next to her friend on the log.

"They've decided," said Naana as a greeting, while she watched the water heat in the gourd.

Keeta got right to the point. "We gave them a spot on

Roanoke Island."

Naana stirred the mixture. "What did Wanchese say?"

Keeta knew word for word what Wanchese had told the council after the wassadors left: "They have crowded out their own land and they want ours. We should never let them get a spot here, for they won't let go until they have all that is ours." But how could she tell this to Naana?

She didn't have to. Naana set the gourd down next to the fire and turned to Keeta. She could barely get out her question: "What about Auwepu?"

Keeta pictured the large men, with their larger appetites, living near their own village and she recoiled from the image. Keeta understood that giving the wassadors a small spot on Roanoke Island was meant to contain them and their influence, but this reasoning would not be soothing for Naana. As much as she searched for comforting words, she could find none. "I don't know," she finally said.

Naana nodded. Keeta knew then her friend had not expected a healing response.

Roanoke Island
Wassadors Settle on Roanoke Island

As Auwepu lowered herself down onto the sand, she shifted the weight of her growing belly backward onto her heels. Placing one hand on the sand for balance, she sifted through the basket of shells with the other. A tall girl with narrow calves waited silently nearby. She watched Auwepu pick through the shells, discarding some and keeping others. Small waves hissed and rolled behind them.

Auwepu looked up and scanned the eastern horizon, now empty of wassador ships. Even the one that had tipped while entering the bay had managed to get straight again and return to the sea. Thinking of the wassadors camped on the other end of the island frightened her, so she turned her attention back to her work.

In marrying Aquandut of Roanoke Island, Auwepu had joined a large, prosperous family, one so important she had left her own family to join her husband's. His family's prestige came from their knowledge and skill in creating the shining beads so widely valued that a string of them could be traded far away, in all directions, save to the east, over the water.

Auwepu had known little about shell polishing. Used to her quiet sister who spoke more often to plants than to people, she worried at first that she had made a mistake in joining this large, boisterous group, a long canoe ride away from Dasemunkepeuc. Bear clan siblings all of them, as a family they were inclined toward industriousness. Easy-going unless provoked, then they became stubborn, intransigent. But Aquandut had shown her only affection, and his family continued to smile and hold her close. They didn't push her to learn their trade any faster than she was able.

Then, one winter's day, after a storm had dragged the sea bottom and spewed its contents, Auwepu and her new cousins had searched the beach for the right shells to transform into beads. Sitting by the warm fire afterwards, Auwepu's basket held the best shells. She basked in the family's admiration. With this encouragement, she began to help with the grinding, first the harsh sand, then the soft sand that polished. Her eye continued to gain notice. She had learned to see what a shell could become. Her role in the family secured, she ceased to feel so ill at ease, and she missed her sister Naana less because of this.

"Nippe," Auwepu held up a piece of the purple-colored mussel shell to the thin-legged girl. "Look at this small crack."

This girl, who now called herself Manunushae Nippe, was the youngest of the Weapemeok women presented to the Roanoke by the wassadors. Four had gone to Roanoke Island, where Kautantowit, as Granganimeo's wife, had spread them around the larger households. The remaining four stayed at Dasemunkepeuc.

Nippe's hair was now styled like the Roanoke, clipped short above the eyes and the sides grown out. Quiet, she had attached herself to Auwepu.

Nippe bent down next to her. Auwepu handed her the shell.

"When we sand it down, the crack will break here," she pointed with her finger, "and here."

Nippe nodded.

As they knelt they heard a loud banging, followed by a series of echoes that felt like waves of compression on their ears. At the sound Nippe stood up straight, her body rigid, her fingers rolled tightly into her palms, her breathing audible.

Then came the piercing cries of the wassador coyotes, tied

to trees in their camp. After only a few days of the wassadors sharing their island, Auwepu already recognized this sound. The other one was new.

Auwepu reached up and unclenched the girl's hand. Nippe had said nothing of what had happened to her, how she had come to be captured by the wassadors, but the other Weapemeok women had spoken of it—the surprise attack, the stick-weapons that could put metal in their enemies and make them bleed, that the wassadors had been uninterested in them as women, and the relief they had felt in being taken to the Roanoke and not across the sea.

Auwepu tugged gently on the girl's hand, pulling her back down to sit. Like she had done with her sister Naana, she tucked the girl's head into her shoulder and stroked her hair. When the girl's chest rose and fell evenly, Auwepu blew lightly on her cheek to tickle her skin. Nippe smiled at this gentle surprise. Then they continued their search of the beach.

Auwepu listened to the wind-driven rain slash against the lodge. Reading the signs—when the gulls flew inland and the rabbits disappeared—the family had secured the roof mats and reinforced their storage caves. Still, as the rain continued, water seeped into the walls, the air turned chilly, and the dampened ground reached from the edges to near the fire in the center of the home. Summer was certainly over. As young girls, she and Naana had enjoyed the storms, passing the time gambling sticks, pretty shells, and rocks. Her new family never played such games. Even the littlest girls picked over shells as the rain continued to flay the mats.

"At least in this rain, we can't hear them taking down all their trees," commented her husband, Aquandut. A garrulous man, he enjoyed conversation, even if he sometimes took both sides of an argument. "Wanchese says that the wassadors have taken down all the trees in their own home. That when a tree grows wider than two hands around, they take it down."

His younger brother Hashap, a master in trapping animals, sat surrounded by a collection of reeds, chiseled sticks, and ropes, the traps he had pulled in before the heavy winds and rain. Tying off a knot, he put down the sticks and questioned his brother. "How can that be? What sense is in a people who would cut down all their trees? And how could they possibly achieve such a thing? The Creator has given us so many trees, who could have enough uses for them?"

"But they don't seem to have any use for what's already been cut. Have you seen how many trees lay felled and un-touched?" Aquandut responded.

Almost everyone on the island had gone to see what the wassadors had constructed, lodges made of halved trees, with no hole in the middle of the roof to vent a fire, or mats to adjust to bring in air or light, and merely one entry. And they had taken down all the trees in the area, regardless of type—not one or two tulip trees for a canoe, not only oak saplings for their dwellings, not fallen, dried pine for their fires, not walnut for their medicines, not witch hazel for their bows, nor ash for their arrows.

Nippe served the stew. Something in her slow, careful manner as she went about ladling the soup into the bowls and handing them one by one to her new family, reminded Auwepu of her sister. From her corner surrounded by warm, dry skins, Auwepu watched how she approached Hashap, how he leaned so slightly so their fingers brushed together as the soup changed hands. He nodded his thanks and then his eyes returned to his work.

"It seems the wassadors can't hunt either. Have you seen them try?" said Aquandut.

Hashap nodded his head, one end of a thin thread wrapped

around his three middle fingers, the other in his mouth.

"They make so much noise that every deer, squirrel, and beaver runs away. If they happen to stumble upon something, they shoot their fire sticks...boom! So anything that hasn't yet run away is running now."

Hashap laughed. His traps took him all around the island and he noticed that the animals had scattered in all directions at the unfamiliar and continual wassador noise. He glanced at Nippe as she ladled stew for the younger ones.

"Why do they keep their animals tied up?" asked Auwepu, who was bothered by their constant complaining.

"If one goes free," said Hashap, "I'll bring it home for dinner."

Aquandut frowned, remembering another thing he had heard from Wanchese, that the wassadors grow their animals like corn, and that the meat doesn't run but stands and waits to be killed. His thoughts were interrupted by Auwepu's laugh.

"They're very fat, they would be delicious," she smiled.

Aquandut turned to look at his beautiful wife, who smiled at him over the fire. "I could cook it with beach plums," she added. "Then it would be sweet."

Dasemunkepeuc
Keeta Makes a Trade

Mishoo's sturdy fingers held his blanket tight in his sleep. In
the early morning half-light, Menuhkeu rubbed his hand over
his son's dark hair, the soft fuzz growing thicker by the day.
This child made Menuhkeu's heart ache in a way he hadn't
known was possible. Even his strong feelings for Keeta had
not produced this powerful urge to protect, to defend. He
smiled at his wife's sleeping figure. Perhaps this was because
his partner was more than able to protect herself.

Menuhkeu began to unwrap himself from the shared blankets, but Keeta reached up and grabbed his hand, pulling
him back.

Menuhkeu wasn't comfortable leaving his small family, but
it was the time to hunt, the time to gather flesh and bones,
and so he had no choice. Usually the hunting parties had
little worry in leaving their village behind. But this year, the
wassadors sat nearby and, if the wind was right, their great
pounding noise flew across the sound, erratic yet ongoing.
The number of warriors was even further reduced because a
group of the wassadors had left Roanoke Island and traveled
up the harbor in their small boats toward Weapemeok territory, and Wingina had sent scouts to trail their movement.

On this morning, the sun had barely risen. A pattern of
interlocking white clouds, shaped like the scales of a silver
bass, lay against the sky. Slivers of blue veined the gray, like
the sea seeping in from behind.

Keeta and Mishoo, with a group of women and their children, were returning from the river. Their hair heavy with moisture and their skin prickled from the chilled bath, the mothers laughed as they hurried toward the fires with their wet children.

Mese, an unmarked boy, raced toward them. "The wassadors are coming!' he shouted. "In their canoes, toward the beach!" He looked from face to face to see that all had taken in his message before he ran off to tell the rest of the village.

"We must flee!" shouted one woman.

"Don't rush to a plan," retorted Keeta before she had a chance to think about her words. As she began to quickly sort their options, she was greatly relieved to see First Mother running down the path.

With a quick motion, First Mother gathered the women around her. "We will hide the stores and prepare to flee," she said. "We don't know what their purpose is, but we must not waste ourselves in fear." She turned to Keeta. "While I prepare the village, go to them. You've been taught to trade. Greet them as if they had come to trade."

Keeta passed Mishoo, wrapped and wriggling in his raccoon pelt, to Minneash.

"Go find Chepeck and Ensenore," First Mother added. "They will help you."

As she ran, Keeta tried to remember which warriors had remained in the village. Her father was gone. Perhaps Asku had stayed behind?

She found Chepeck wrapped in a buffalo blanket near a warm fire, his long hair unadorned, bent fingers holding the edges of the skin together to keep in the heat. Shaggy and brown and big, the animal that gave this skin lived far away and it was the only blanket of its kind in Dasemunkepeuc. The spirit guide's busy household bustled around him, preparing to flee. Despite her inner feelings of worry, Keeta offered respectful greetings.

"We will greet the visitors," Chepeck advised. "And don't forget, there are still many warriors on Roanoke Island."

Keeta nodded.

"Manteo isn't here to explain that a visit wasn't expected, but we must greet them as allies. Father Ensenore will preside. If they've come to trade, you have been taught the ways and if they come for other reasons, you will be able to keep your head."

Keeta at once remembered being a girl and sitting with her family as she told them the vision the ancestors had given her. Then, Wanchese had told her some years later that she was capable of more strength than she knew, and that she would be called to carry her people on her back. "Yes, father," she answered Chepeck. "I will do this."

Keeta waited for the visitors with Chepeck, hidden behind a lodge. She felt only curiously alert until the five of them showed up at the greeting area, guided from the beach by Asku. Then she had to make herself breathe in the power of the Creator to remind herself who she was.

Two wassadors wore soft clothes, the others their suits of metal. Ensenore, copper bracelets on his arms, greeted them. He bid two boys to start a small fire and sat down. Two wassadors sat, but the other three, the ones in metal, remained standing. The Roanoke boys close to their moon trek spun the maple stick onto the cedar. The dry moss became flame. When Ensenore pulled out his old appowac pouch, beaded with purple shells and decorated with two coyote feet, Chepeck and Keeta joined the group and sat.

To resist the urge to stare at the newcomers sitting only feet away, Keeta watched Ensenore as he put a generous pinch of appowac into his pipe. Ensenore inhaled deeply and then passed it around, to Chepeck, to Keeta, to the visitors. As they reached to take the smoking pipe, Keeta, her heart pounding and her thoughts moving more rapidly with the appowac, regarded them.

They certainly resembled men, despite their white skin and odd smell. She recognized the seated ones—the sharp-chinned one, Harriot, who spoke Roanoke words, and White, the one so round it was as if his bones were padded in skins, carrying his large bag. Their posture wasn't quiet, nor balanced. Even the silent ones who stood behind had their bodies always in motion, with unpredictable twists and shifting, so that Asku, on guard, was again and again near to reaching for his club in defense and then putting his arms down again.

Ensenore greeted them with words of welcome.

Wequassus arrived with what she could find on no warn-ing, a portion of dried bluefish and some corn. The seated wassadors ate quickly and in large gulps. The ones standing watched the food with greedy eyes. Ever the gracious host, Wequassus served them as well, even though no Roanoke would eat standing up.

Despite Keeta's place in the circle, the wassadors didn't once look directly at her or acknowledge her presence. She wondered at this, but it gave her more opportunity to ob-serve, and her nerves calmed. She began to wonder what the Roanoke might gain from this visit rather than worrying about what might be lost.

Harriot bared his teeth, like a wolf or a coyote, and tried what may have been Roanoke words. Then he clapped his hands twice, sideways, right over left, left over right.

Ensenore looked to Chepeck and Keeta before he spoke and they nodded in agreement—so clearly did Harriot make the signs of trade, they couldn't pretend to not understand. "We are eager to help, to be of service to you, our powerful friends," Ensenore replied to Harriot's request.

Harriot held up his arm and curled his fingers around,

turning them this way and that, speaking something, a word Keeta didn't understand. He then pointed at Ensenore's upper arm, at his bracelet. Ensenore pointed to his bracelet and the wassador nodded his approval. Perhaps he wanted the bracelet? Keeta wondered. By this point, all the Roanoke had heard of the wassadors' love for metal.

Sharp-chinned Harriot's next words were clearly Roanoke. "Squash," he might have said, and then "beans" and "corn" and "meat." No one answered. So odd was this request for food just after he had been served, and at a time when food was so plentiful. He picked up his bowl and pretended to eat.

"I think he wants to trade for part of our crop," said Keeta quietly, unsure of how much Harriot understood. "They prefer squash, and beans, and possibly meat."

When Keeta said squash, he nodded.

"Such a strange request! Could they really want meat, during the hunting season?" whispered Ensenore. "It must be some kind of trick."

Keeta thought of how they ate, bowl after bowl until food was no longer offered. Even when we have plenty, she thought, we are saving for when we have nothing. No one would eat like that, as if the bowl were never ending. Keeta tried to understand their wants, how were they planning to get through the winter? Yet, they didn't look hungry or desperate. Not at all.

It struck her then that this was an opportunity. She knew exactly what the Roanoke had, how full the storage caves were. She turned to Ensenore. "Tell them we want the metal tool, the one they used to take down all their trees."

Ensenore explained, using his hands to mimic a tree falling, but the wassadors were confused. The padded one, White, reached for his bag and pulled out of it a pile of large white leaves without veins. Flat, smooth and shaped like a mat, they were of a bright material Keeta had never seen before. On this he traced a stick that left marks, like a stick on sand or dirt.

The Roanoke who, once they had chosen not to immediately flee, had stood back until this moment, now moved forward to see. With his stick, White made some lines. He pointed to a tree and then at his white leaf. He traced what looked like a tree on his leaf, and then he traced an object, placing it at the side of the tree on his leaf: it was a tool to cut down the tree. He held it up and Keeta ran her fingers over the image, something like the markings on a pot or a canoe or a skin bag. She had to fight not to be distracted by these white leaves and worked to consider how many baskets of beans she should offer for the metal object. Ensenore and Chepeck watched and said nothing. The crowd that had gathered began to murmur.

White too seemed distracted by the success of his leaves. With his stick he next made an image of the nearest lodge to the meeting circle, the one owned by the family of Namohs, masters at weir building. Their lodge sat on his leaf. Several children then ran to Namohs lodge and back to White to make sure one hadn't replaced the other, so real were the markings. White, who knew nothing of Roanoke words, looked up from his work to smile and nod at those around him in a way that made the children who were bravest rush in to see what he was doing. Gradually, all were comfortable standing close to him to see him work his leaves and sticks. He made in this way the boy Mese, working quickly with his sticks until the boy appeared. Mese didn't fully comprehend what had happened until he was told and then he stared at his image and laughed, full of pride. Still some touched Mese and then the page to make sure that one hadn't taken the other.

White then pulled out other leaves, with other images already captured. A field of corn, a striped bass, a turtle, and then, coming out of the page Keeta saw Auwepu, her face round and belly full of child. She cried out to see her friend like this and worried that Auwepu had gone to another world, even as she saw that Mese stood by at the same time he was on the white leaves. The images were so real to life. Keeta sat back and closed her eyes, and her mind wandered to Naana. Naana, who spent more and more of her time in the woods with Wautog, was not among the gathered crowd and Keeta was glad of it.

She pulled her thoughts back in. Manteo had said there was much to learn from these people. The tool Pog had taken was so helpful. She opened her eyes.

"Two metal tree-takers," Keeta said. "We want two for a basket of beans and squash, and two deer." Ensenore started to protest, but Chepeck stopped him with a soft word. The wassadors agreed to these terms.

The day on its wane, the wassadors retreated to Roanoke Island in their canoes. Mese's laughter travelled the village as he told and retold all who would listen how he had been captured by the wassador and put onto a leaf. Keeta did not share his glee. When she recalled the boy's thin image and the one of Auwepu, it felt as if they had been stolen somehow and were already on their way to another place. Although Keeta had traded corn and beans and squash, she couldn't shake the feeling she had traded Auwepu and Mese. Then, the two metal tools no longer felt like such a bargain.

Dasemunkepeuc
Naana Searches for Plants During the Hunting Moon

Naana and Wautog set out when the sun peeked out as a pinch of red in the east. The hunting moon, the time just before the earth turns hard and unyielding and most blooms have dried and blown away, was a rich time for gathering roots.

Since the end of the second corn harvest, a small boy, son of the fish driers, had been accompanying Wautog and Naana on their gatherings. At first the boy, Chogen, followed wordlessly, waiting for them at the end of the path in the early morning. After several weeks, Naana began to name the plants they took and show him how and where to take bark from a tree. When he remembered what he had been shown, Wautog taught him the proper thanks and blessings.

Today, the three had separated early. On the western side of a large boulder, Naana came upon a late patch of golden asters, yellow flowers gone, leaves turning into the ground. She scooped her clamshell around the shrinking aster plant to loosen the soil and free the roots. As she worked she thanked the plant for its medicine, a gentle cure particularly well suited for infants and young children. Careful not to break any of the spreading roots, she lifted them out, wrapped them in a leaf, and placed them in her basket. This spot had given her asters two years running, and so she made sure to leave enough roots to grow for next year.

She stood and went to find Wautog. The younger woman still accompanied the older as often as she could, for there were always new things to learn, hidden caches, tips on how to read the soil. Over the past year, Wautog had grown very thin, and she had begun to lose the ability to see with precision. Still, she had strength for long treks, and her will to have a good supply of all that was needed for the village had not weakened. Some claimed it was the loss of her own children to sickness that drove her, but Naana knew that Wautog's motivation was not death, but life: the act of guiding a new spirit from between the legs of a mother was what gave the medicine woman her fire.

Naana found her, along with Chogen, toward the swamps, peering down.

Wautog called Naana over. "Look," she whispered, pointing to a sharp-leaved, low-lying plant whose red berries had fallen. The older woman knelt heavily on the forest floor. Naana and the boy knelt beside her.

Pulling some appowac out of her shoulder pouch, she pinched some between her dirt-blackened fingers and said a blessing. She took Chogen's hand in hers, guiding his fingers into the dirt. Together they dug for a twisted root, many inches below the surface. With the dirt loosened, Wautog pulled on the plant to withdraw it whole.

The woman held up the root and chuckled. Its two melded sides crossed over, like legs under a torso. "Man root," she said as she handed it to the boy. "A very good find."

Naana regarded its tan color, its many thin tendrils trailing away from the center. Chogen brought it to his nose and sniffed.

"Very powerful," continued Wautog. "You can trade it, but..."

"It's best not to let others know you have it," answered Naana.

The boy turned to her, and something about his serious, thin face searching for the meaning of her words struck Naana as too old for his years. She wondered perhaps if his odd inclination to follow them into the woods was an example of an old spirit entering an infant's body at birth, as she had heard sometimes occurred.

Later, she knew that it must be so, and that the Spirit had sent help when they needed it the most.

Roanoke Island
A Visit to the Wassador Camp

Menuhkeu and Asku met Aquandut on the far side of Roanoke Island. Together they pulled up the canoes and unloaded the baskets of beans and squash, and two deer. Aquandut explained what those on the island had quickly learned. "If you wait, you'll hear it," he said. "They're tied by metal ropes to the ground." Although a little older, Aquandut had always been friendly to the younger warriors, joking and including them in his conversations. As they looped the baskets onto a long pole so they could easily be carried with a person on each end, Menuhkeu heard the animal's cry, like a coyote, but sharper, deeper.

"Do you hear that?" said Aquandut. "That's why they can't hunt. Their animals scare all the game away."

"I hear they can't hunt anywhere else either," answered Menuhkeu. "Their fire sticks have no aim."

"Gun," corrected Aquandut. "They call it a gun."

"Gun," attempted Asku.

"How could they come here without food? Or a way to get food?" asked Menuhkeu.

"They claim the ship that Memegwasi tipped had their food in it," said Granganimeo, as he approached. In Manteo's absence, Granganimeo had become quite adept at interpreting what it was the wassadors wanted to say.

The younger warriors greeted Granganimeo, and sent Wingina's regards.

"Their weroance, this man Lane, is by nature suspicious," warned Granganimeo, as they made their way to the camp.

"Their customs are very different, so make no sudden movements. They might be misjudged."

They approached Lane's village from a path through the pines, the younger men carrying the food. The strange barking of their animals echoed in the tall timbers.

The denuded wassador area came into view; where trees had stood now pooled black puddles from the recent rain. Granganimeo stopped and held up his hand, quiet. The warriors stopped behind him.

Although several boatloads of wassadors had left for Weapemeoc territory at the end of summer and had not returned, many numbers of them remained here, on the tip of Roanoke Island. Menuhkeu regarded the large enclosure constructed from hewn timbers, shaped into sharp points at the top and planted deep into the ground, and was reminded of the protected Pomeioc village. Unlike the Pomeioc village, however, square structures made of cut wood and various metal objects stood outside the pointed fence. Menuhkeu wondered at the power of these objects, and the trouble to bring them so far across the water.

His attention was quickly diverted, however, by an event a little further away.

A wassador, stripped of his shirt, knelt on the ground. His hands, tied together, were pulled up by a rope that hung from a branch above. Their weroance, Lane, recognizable by his thick body and the way the others deferred to him, circled around the kneeling man, holding a long rope. He spoke forcefully as a group of wassadors stood back at a distance and watched. The animals continued their barking, loudly and at intervals.

Menuhkeu turned to Asku; the kneeling man's posture made them both uneasy. Was this some kind of ceremony? Some test of strength?

Lane brought the rope down on the man's back. The man

cried out. If this was a test of strength, thought Menuhkeu, it must be near the end, for him to cry out like that. A thin pink line turned red on his skin. They bleed like us, he concluded. Lane brought his arm over his head and then down, lashing the man's back again. After two more strokes, he handed the rope to another wassador, who continued to strike the man. Lane turned and walked away.

The Roanoke, at pains not to interrupt the rite, remained at the edge of the clearing. Lane looked up and noticed them, so Granganimeo strode forward.

Harriot hurried over. This sharp-chinned man knew Roanoke words, Keeta had warned Menuhkeu and Asku before they left. "Come, come," Harriot urged them, as he gestured toward an area away from the rite.

Granganimeo glanced at the bleeding man, prostate now on the dirt, his back running with the blood of many stripes.

"The man did a bad thing," said Harriot.

The warriors exchanged glances. A weroance who injures his own warriors?

Harriot watched their faces. He didn't offer his visitors a place of rest or something to eat. By this time, though, Menuhkeu knew not to expect this. The wassadors were not good hosts.

Lane approached the group, coming into Menuhkeu's line of sight. Menuhkeu took advantage of this opportunity to study Lane. Without his metal suit, the pink flesh at his neck looked vulnerable. Menuhkeu noted the man's strength as well, the broad chest and insistent, thrusting belly.

At Granganimeo's nod, Menuhkeu and Asku slipped the baskets off the carrying pole. Aquandut placed the deer next to the baskets, slipping out the pole with one motion.

Lane glanced at the bundles on the ground with no expression on his face save a few twitches at the corner of his mouth. His fingers curled and uncurled briefly into his palm before he spoke a few words to Harriot, who nodded and turned to Granganimeo.

Lane spoke again.

"Corn," Harriot said. "We want corn."

Menuhkeu recognized the word. He looked fifty yards in the distance to where the ceremony had now stopped, the many wassadors dispersing. How was it that they were so powerful, with their many objects of wassador, and had no corn?

Granganimeo pointed to the baskets and to the deer, but the wassadors struggled to interpret his intention.

Menuhkeu knew that Granganimeo couldn't promise corn, even if he wanted to, without consulting his wife. Women were in charge of the corn, the storage, the distribution, and the planting. Only they knew what was needed and what could be spared. And corn was rarely traded; if it was given, it was given in tribute.

"Corn," Harriot repeated. Once again, Granganimeo pointed to all they had brought.

After some words with Harriot, at last Lane nodded his acceptance of the provisions.

"Manteo?" Harriot asked.

"No," replied Granganimeo, shaking his head and pointing down the coast to south, in the direction of Croatoan, where the translator was visiting his family.

Harriot nodded his understanding, and turned to poke through the carcasses, using their words for each part of the deer and then asking for the Roanoke words. Lane stood nearby, shifting on his feet.

The Roanoke warriors, following Granganimeo's lead, merely nodded and pointed. Keeta's warning aside, Menuhkeu felt a danger in giving over too much to these people.

A wassador returned with a bag. "Hatchet," said Harriot, who pulled the tool out of the bag and handed it to Lane, who in turn passed it to Granganimeo, wood end first. Menuhkeu followed Lane's eyes. They were light, like the color of the ocean in winter.

"Hatchet," repeated Harriot, clearly wanting the Roanoke word for the object. No one answered him, this time not because of protection or shyness or obstinacy, but because they had no word for the thick handled tool, with its sharp, heavy metal head.

Granganimeo took the hatchet and handed it to Aquandut. He held up his finger, one more. Harriot reached again into the bag and the second hatchet was passed to Lane, and then to Granganimeo.

Granganimeo handed this second hatchet to Menuhkeu, who noted with pleasure the heft of it in his hand, the sharpness of the blade, suddenly proud that Keeta had thought to bargain for it.

On the walk back, Menuhkeu passed Asku the hatchet. He noticed, though, that Granganimeo and Aquandut were less gleeful at the new tool, even though no Roanoke Island food was used to procure it. When the canoes were pulled off the sand and the Dasemunkepeuc warriors ready to leave, the weroance at last spoke his mind. "We cannot feed them throughout the winter."

Asku looked up in surprise. "Of course not," he answered, confused.

Menuhkeu looked at Aquandut's grim face, a man so often laughing or talking, and he understood. Of course the Roanoke could not keep another village throughout the winter—no tribe would expect that. The wassadors, however, would not know this. It was clear that the wassadors understood nothing of what it was to survive here.

Dasemunkepeuc
Pog Falls Ill

When Menuhkeu arrived at Pog's family lodge, the crowd already spilled out the door, and a small group was gathered on sitting rocks, chanting healing songs. He squeezed his way inside, where Pog laid on the bench near the fire, his mother on one side and Wautog on the other. Menuhkeu nearly retreated out the door in surprise when he saw how his friend had changed since he had last seen him, two days ago, when they had returned from hunting. Pog tossed from side to side, half-awake, his skin dry and gray, like ash tree bark. Pog's mother was a garrulous woman of strong arms and back, and Menuhkeu knew her well from the many times she had ministered medicine to others. Her open ways and calm manner made her easy company to the sick. Her manner now sober, she sat by her son and recited to Wautog what she had given him—drinks of steeped coneflower and lobelia, over the last day and a half. This combination had worked at first, she recited, his heat had lessened, but then sores, like soft bubbles, appeared in his throat and mouth. She had never seen anything like this before and hoped that Wautog, in all her wisdom, could advise them.

Pog had been Menuhkeu's steady companion since childhood, like a brother to Menuhkeu, whose brothers were older, more like uncles. He knelt by his friend, who sat half up and vomited into a gourd held up by his mother.

"Pog," he said softly.

"The sores in his mouth make it difficult for him to speak," said Wautog, but Menuhkeu felt his friend didn't recognize him.

"Do you have any man root?" Wautog asked Pog's mother. She shook her head no.

"I'll get you some," Wautog replied. The woman pushed herself up, hands on knees. Menuhkeu took her elbow to steady her.

"Let me help you, grandmother," he said.

Still, by the next day, the bubbles had made their way out Pog's mouth and onto his face, traveling quickly down his neck and torso and then out to his arms and legs, until there remained barely any unblemished skin. As the days passed, the bubbles expanded with yellow water and then hardened, round and firm, like small beads under the skin. Wautog steamed witch-hazel into a tincture to apply to his sores, but they failed to respond. By then, Pog was unrecognizable. By then, Menuhkeu could no longer visit his friend, as the sickness spread to other lodges.

One after the other, Pog's family fell ill: his mother, his father, his sisters, their husbands, his five nieces and nephews.

Dasemunkepeuc
Mama Falls Ill

Keeta looked up from the fire as Menuhkeu stepped into its light. From his face, covered in sadness, she knew her answer before he sat close by her and took her hand in his. "He looked...like, like someone who was already dead."

It was strange for someone like Pog to fall sick like that, all at once. Keeta leaned into Menuhkeu. The warmth and strength of him gave her such comfort. She closed her eyes.

"And Wautog, when I walked back to her lodge with her, she told me that she had never seen any sickness like it before."

At the sound of footsteps, Keeta opened her eyes. Her father appeared. The expression of Adchaen's face resembled her husband's.

"Your mother," he said, his voice hoarse. "She isn't well."

Keeta found her mother, arms hanging down off the bench on which she lay, skin on fire, confused. It pained her to see her mother like this, uncomfortable, her words without meaning. And she looked old, her skin loose and dry, her limbs weak. Keeta boiled teas of coneflower and lobelia to ease the fever. She sat with her, and helped her to sip these drinks, leaving her mother with others only when she took a break to go and feed Mishoo, whom she had left in the care of Minneash. But her mother's skin turned to bark, her hair stuck to the sides of her head, and her arms became too weak to lift her hands to her face.

By the second day, her Mama's mouth was swollen with

bubbles. Keeta began to hear of others falling sick with the same fever, and, with so many ill, there were fewer and fewer to help. Keeta felt so worn and yet also so anxious that she couldn't rest, too worried to leave her mother even to sleep for a little. She waved Menuhkeu away, and she began to fear that her mother was dying, that this was the last of the time they would have together. This filled her with such an agony of feeling that she pushed it down and focused on keeping her mother's head on soft skins and helping her sip her healing teas.

On the third day, the illness took a turn for the worse. When the bubbles crawled out her mouth and across his wife's beautiful face, Adchaen cried. Soon her arms, her legs, between her fingers, were covered with raw, red balls that became hard.

Naana visited with a tincture of witch hazel, but there were so many of these sores that there was little comfort in the medicine.

At times, Mama opened her eyes and seemed to see her daughter, her husband. Then Keeta sang the song Mama had taught the children, when she held them in her arms, when she named the birds with them, when she splashed their toes in the waters. Adchaen and Menuhkeu and First Mother and the others visiting in the lodge joined in: "We are the stars that sing, we sing with our light; we are the birds of fire, we fly over the sky. Our light is a voice; we make a road for the spirits; for the spirits to pass over."

But mostly the illness held her. By the fifth night, Mama could no longer open her eyes, but one time she moved her lips. Keeta bent her ear to her mouth. "Kiatee," she said, her voice rough and thick. Kiatee, the special name she had not used when Keeta was young, a name she had not used for many years. Keeta knew then her mother was ready to join Keeta's sisters and brothers, as the Spirit took back all his children.

At this, Keeta felt as lost as she ever had. Only the cries of Mishoo, which set her milk moving again, allowed her to have the strength to look away from her Mama and stand up, and to turn her back on the body. And then her thoughts were dark.

Dasemunkepeuc
Naana Searches for a Cure

Naana knelt over a bubbling brew in Wautog's small lodge, gently stirring. The healer's lodge held the remaining supply of medicine. Dried roots, plants, and barks lined the walls, hung from the roof, were tucked in small deerskin pouches or larger covered baskets, or were buried in the earth. Wautog herself was no longer there—her body had been stored for some days now in the back of the death lodge with the others, waiting to be wrapped.

It was late in the night, but Naana had barely slept since the first marks appeared on Pog. She had spent her days helping Wautog boil down plants, traveling with her to the lodges to show the people how to apply the medicine and then, when Wautog became ill, caring for the old woman. With so many ill, it became impossible to care for every sick person, but still Naana continued making the medicine and bringing it to the sickest lodges. She worried about her sister Auwepu on Roanoke Island, whether they had the disease as well, whether her sister had fallen ill and, if so, who was caring for her.

The boy Chogen knelt nearby, amidst bundles of plants. In the flickering light of the cooking fire, he and Naana were taking an accounting of the diminished stocks, searching out substitutes for lobelia, which was in short supply, and man root, which had been consumed. Chogen reached toward a basket pushed under the bench. Inside was a collection of roots from the wetlands, gathered just before the frost.

He pulled it out and examined its contents. So far, Chogen

had lost his two uncles, his grandmother, and his two younger sisters. His eyes were red from crying and deeply circled, but still he worked with Naana, searching the forests, stirring the boiling plants.

He held up a root. Uncertain of its origin, he asked, "Pitcher plant?"

Naana took the root. Rarely used, it served as a back up for a collection of different plants—it seemed to help the sick person weather an illness, but its effects weren't predictable, sometimes making the person weaker by inducing vomiting or diarrhea.

By the freshness of the strings, Naana could tell that Wautog had tied this large bundle together recently. Maybe there was something in the plant that made her think it might be worth trying. Naana hesitated. Wautog wouldn't try a plant out for a new purpose without guidance. "We'll bring it to Chepeck, so that the Creator can guide our choice," the girl decided. She put the bundle in her pouch and the two left to find Chepeck.

They met him in the village. Chepeck had aged deeply over the last few weeks. On little sleep, he shook his precious turtle shell rattle and sang songs of healing over his people, the sacred melodies taught to him, the same chants his ancestors had received from Nanabohzo, who in turn had received them from the Creator.

Chepeck's arms hung listlessly, and his rabbit cloak seemed to fall lower on his thin legs than it had just a few short days ago. The spirit leader greeted them with soft words, and together the three walked silently to his lodge, where Chepeck fueled the embers. They sat as the flames licked the dark, as he threw the appowac. Chepeck closed his eyes.

Naana closed her eyes as well. She tried not to think of Chogen's sisters, so small, so covered with the creeping red blisters that the tincture of witch hazel she had smoothed over them had made them gasp as it hit their skin. They hadn't lasted very long, the sisters, and the two had passed almost at the same time.

Naana felt herself drifting, but not with sleep. In this state she found herself at the swamp where she had gathered the pitcher plant back in the fall. The plants were noisy, not whispering quietly as they usually do, but gurgling and thrusting their voices up to her. Without opening her eyes, she related this to Chepeck as she saw the images running across her mind.

"Yes," replied Chepeck. "The Creator has given us a gift to help us in this sickness." He paused before continuing. "Use the root of the plant as soon as the fever hits. The poison of the disease is so great that it needs greater poison to counter it."

He lowered the fire and the three returned to Wautog's lodge, where they worked through the night in boiling down the swamp root into a tea they could give to the people.

Dasemunkepeuc
Keeta Falls Ill

Keeta felt them form on the roof of her mouth, weak places where the skin responded too easily to the touch of her tongue, raw spots that quickly multiplied. As the fire ran through her, the heat sent sharp pains through her back and head so that she could not move, nor form words. Sores covered her and then broke, leaving her skin oozing with yellow pus. Even a rush of air hitting her open skin brought a pulse of pain, and she jarred herself time after time with her own shallow breathing. Menuhkeu sat with her, pulling at her spirit to stay.

Still, she went away from him. Keeta went swimming under water, going a long distance, until the great panther appeared, a dark shadow chasing her from behind. She ducked away, into a tunnel that led into a narrow cave that was warm and dry. Climbing into it, she could see a small hole at the far end of the cave that let in sunshine, bright like a summer's day. Through this hole, Keeta saw so many people coming toward her—Pog, Mama, Wunne Wadsh and her oldest son, Wautog, Chogen's two sisters, and the small boy who loved canoes, Mese. And then, making her way first through the crowd, she saw Auwepu, full with her child. Keeta reached out her hand out to rub the belly. "No," Auwepu stopped her hands. The others came closer. Keeta wanted to see them. Auwepu shook her head, "No!"

Keeta didn't want to listen. She wanted to hold her Mama. Auwepu became insistent. "You don't belong here!" she said, glancing back as the others ventured closer, their arms out.

Keeta begged Auwepu to let her pass, for she so wanted to go to that sunny world. But, as the people approached, Keeta felt the chill of them. Mama became smaller and harder to find in the crowd. "See?" said Auwepu, her gentle face full of sadness. "It is not your time." She pushed Keeta out of the cave and into the water, and Keeta had no choice but to swim back.

Back from the world between, Keeta felt pain where she lay on the deerskin, the throbbing inside her head. She heard the soft songs of Menuhkeu and the voice of Naana as she entered her lodge with her basket of medicine. Keeta opened her eyes.

"I have something new for her to try," Naana said to Menuhkeu. "She will be the first one to try it, but the plant is sure it can help."

Dasemunkepeuc
Naana is Overcome

When she learned of her sister's death, Naana threw herself into the sea to swim to Roanoke Island to reach Auwepu's body. Standing on the beach, Chogen was sure the water panther Mishibijiw would take Naana for his own, so he called to Asku, nearby in the ancestor trees, where he mourned the passing of his own sisters.

Naana hadn't swum too far when Asku reached her. Even as a woman, Naana was as slight as a girl, and she was so distraught that Asku easily scooped her up, swam her in, wrapped her in his deerskin cloak and carried her back to the village in his arms like a child. She did not speak, but stayed limp in his arms, her head turned into his chest. She had found the plant that calmed the sickness too late.

Naana said later that the steady pumping of Asku's heart as he walked with her in his arms convinced her own heart to start working again.

And Asku told Menuhkeu that he hadn't heard Chogen's cries for help at all, and that if he had it would have been too late anyway. It was his sisters' urging him from the ancestor trees to get up from his sorrow, to go and find someone to accompany him in this world. On their instructions, he went to the beach and saw Naana enter the waves.

Dasemunkepeuc
Keeta Visits the Death Lodge

The overpowering smell greeted Keeta before she even entered the death lodge with Chepeck. Little of the low fall afternoon light made its way into the high-ceilinged lodge, the place where the drained and wrapped bodies of the Roanoke dead were kept until their flesh left and their bones buried. Keeta adjusted her breathing and steadied herself.

The sickness had coursed its way so rapidly through the village that it had been difficult for the overwhelmed families to take all the necessary steps to lead the spirits to the world of the dead. Not all the bodies were drained fully and sewn into their own deerskin pouches. Some families had bundled the children together, and some bodies were merely covered with skins, not yet sewn or drained.

And many hadn't yet been sung on to their next destination. Keeta's Mama, a woman with an open heart and the caretaker of many children, had been sung on, but Chepeck agreed that a mother sung on by her living daughter will have the most comfort in the land of the dead, so Keeta, when she healed, returned to the death lodge to perform that kindness for her Mama.

Chepeck had laid the body, a small deerskin-wrapped bundle, next to a low fire. A strong urge to pry open the seams, to make sure this was her mother and to see her one last time, possessed Keeta, but she knew this urge came from the unsettled spirits of the dead, not yet properly attended to, confused, sometimes greedy and destructive, lingering and interfering with the living. She pushed the image of her mother's sick body away and focused on her spirit.

Keeta remembered the closeness of sleeping, the feeling of her back warmed by her mother's embrace, arms wrapping her close during wet winter nights, her Mama's breath warming her face. She remembered the pull of her scalp while her Mama combed nut oil through her hair. Throughout her girlhood, Keeta fingered the blue flowers on her skirt. Today, she ran her fingers over the linked loops on her arm, the inkings of a person too old to sleep with her Mama, a person with her own child to care for.

Keeta's heart warmed, and the sensation of her Mama flooded through her. With this came sorrow, but also a new kind of strength, of power. She sang her goodbyes, wishing her mother a gentle journey, an easy transition.

"Go Nunnootam," Chepeck sang. "You who cared for so many can now be cared for."

They sang a long time. They sang until Keeta knew that her mother could go away, to where she now belonged, to the other world, the dead world.

She sat back from the body and regarded the spirit guide in the low light.

Chepeck came from a long line of herring-clan keepers of the dead, the job going usually from grandfather to grandson, and so he was related to both Keeta and her mother. Her mother had stitched rabbit skins into the cloak he now wore. When Keeta left, he would lift the bundle that was her mother, resting it on his shoulders to climb the ladder up to the rack. There, he would set the wrapped body with the others, where it would stay until the bones could be buried, in a spot away from the sea, with the rest of the Roanoke people.

"Shall I stay and sing some of the other spirits on?" Keeta asked, remembering how insistent they had been, crowding through the hole in the cave to come to her, to touch her, until Auwepu had told her to go back. Auwepu, from the land of the dead, had known that her sister Naana had found the plant that would lessen the illness so that the strong ones could survive.

Chepeck nodded his assent to Keeta's request. He threw some appowac onto the low flames and began the song that told the dead spirits how to go to their ancestors. He chanted strongly and firmly, and Keeta followed his lead. She felt the confusion of the dead whose families hadn't been able to properly conduct their relatives into the next world, and she calmed them. She told them to follow her Mama to the bright, always-summer world.

When she could sing no more, she left the lodge of the dead.

In the chilly night, Menuhkeu stood waiting a short distance away. Keeta walked toward him and took his hand, and together they returned home. Along the way, the lodges that hadn't been abandoned had the glow of fire inside, and the night was quiet and dark.

Dasemunkepeuc
The Roanoke Take Stock

Owush hesitated at the entrance to the lodge. Menuhkeu saw how his brother avoided looking at Keeta, her skin speckled with barely closed red welts. Close to death when Naana delivered the new medicine and still weak, Keeta sat busy braiding reeds to fix a hole in a basket and didn't appear aware of Owush's discomfort.

"Brother," Owush said. "Our father is waiting."

Menuhkeu nodded.

"I'm ready," prompted Keeta.

The three walked in silence, the only sound from the too-quiet village the scraping of dried leaves shuttling in the sea wind.

Wingina's lodge was crowded with people from both Dasemunkepeuc and Roanoke Island. Menuhkeu nodded to Aquandut, whom he'd last seen when they'd collected the promised hatchets from the wassadors, a kizi ago. Also seated were Granganimeo and Wanchese. That each of the three men lost his wife to the wassador's illness and that everyone else had lost at least one relative silenced the usual pre-council banter.

Sitting down with the young warriors, near Asku, Menuhkeu sharply felt Pog's absence. Wampeikuc nodded to his sons from his place next to Wingina. Keeta settled in next to First Mother.

Chepeck readied himself to give the counting by throwing a pinch of appowac on the fire. Menuhkeu noticed how deep, curved grooves now lined the sides of the healer's face. Eyes closed, head back, the keeper of the dead recited: "seventy-two at Dasemunkepeuc, fifty-three at Roanoke Island, and sixty-eight at Croatoan Island."

Wingina, head bent, listened to the numbers.

"The Secotan lost two hundred and fifteen, the Weapemeok one hundred forty-seven, and the Choanoak ninety-eight."

The fire crackled. A barred owl hooted. Menuhkeu's heart raced as if something inside him were trying to crawl its way free. "How many wassadors died?" he burst out.

A quick look from his father stopped Menuhkeu from continuing, but he could feel the tension in the lodge. He had spoken for the majority.

Chepeck sighed, a deep and reflective thrust of air. "None."

Ensenore raised his arms in anger, fox claws hanging off his wrists. "What kind of question is that? We know the wassadors sent the invisible poison arrows to us!"

"Why did they send us poison arrows?" questioned Granganimeo, his voice rising. "We gave them a place for their camp. We let them take their canoes through our waters, and we traded with them for food."

"They have crowded out their own home and so they want ours," warned Wanchese. "They want everything that is ours."

"They have weapons beyond what we even know is possible. What will happen to us if we don't give them all the food they want, and more?" countered Ensenore.

First Mother turned to him. "Our numbers are so diminished that we have plenty of food to spare. We can give them all they want. Maybe that was their plan all along, to get rid of us, to take our food."

"Because they can't manage to get any on their own," said Aquandut. "I will tell you," he began in his storyteller's voice and Menuhkeu found himself leaning in to listen, as if to a hunting tale. "You know my brother Hashap, whose traps are all over the island."

Murmurs of assent came from those seated. Hashap's traps were well regarded by both villages.

"He sets his traps about Roanoke Island in a precise system. A trap doesn't sit too long in the same place, and each is checked regularly so that the setting and the collecting and the resetting forms a circle of motion that results in a steady supply of meat."

How funny we are, thought Menuhkeu. So many terrible things, yet we are all ready to hear a good story.

"Two days ago, the morning had already yielded a beaver whose skull had been crushed by a falling cascade of heavy stones. Three squirrels caught into a small-hole net, quickly quieted, found a home on Hashap's belt."

There were some acknowledgments of the good haul, of the skill of Hashap from Aquandut's audience. "But at the next trap, a collection of leaves and twine, he saw that something had clearly sprung the trap. But no animal was waiting at the bottom of the deep hole. And at the next, a bloody wooden block sat below a branch, but there was no sign of an animal, wounded or eaten. All the traps on the west end were empty." He waited to let this news sink in—four sprung traps, traces of blood in some, and nothing caught.

The west end was the wassador end of Roanoke Island. Aquandut's words lingered while the listeners digested their meaning.

Menuhkeu exchanged glances with Asku. Only an enemy takes from another's trap.

"Thank you for that story," praised Wingina. "That they want food makes it more certain they are men, like us." He paused. "That they are not our friends is certain. That they are uncertain allies is also clear." He paused again. "We know they can't feed themselves. We know they love metal."

Menuhkeu remembered the interest Harriot had shown in Ensenore's copper bracelets.

"Yes," agreed Wanchese. "They love all things metal."

"Maybe this is a weakness. We don't yet know. And until we know how to best defeat them," said Wingina, "we should trade them food," he suggested. "We cannot risk losing any more of our people to their poison arrows. When we go to trade with Menatonon and the Choanoak, and the Weapemeok, we will consult with them."

Menuhkeu glanced over at Keeta who, head down, was fingering her inkings. Since her mother's death, this had become a habit.

No one voiced disagreement to this plan. Yet the Roanoke left the council unsatisfied with the wise choice because, in truth, it did not reflect their collective anger.

Dasemunkepeuc; Through Weapemeok Territory to
Choanoak Territory
Keeta and the Roanoke Trading Party Pay Another Visit to
Menatonon

Keeta's view shifted from sightless dark to a tender gray
as the rising sun's light crept into the lodge. She watched
Menuhkeu turn in his sleep toward Mishoo, who slept between them. Her husband's steady breaths blew the soft
rabbit hairs of their blanket toward Mishoo's cheek, and
Mishoo's nose crinkled in response.

Deep into winter, cold clung to the air. As Keeta slipped
out of the warm cocoon, she tucked the rabbit skin around
Mishoo and the length of her husband so that the chill could
not creep in. The three of them would travel far today, but
Keeta stopped her thoughts from going too far forward.
Instead, she settled herself and started a small fire to reheat
the last of the stew, which didn't travel well. Ground corn for
the trip she had already sewn into leather pouches, enough
to carry them to Choanoak territory and back.

The fire took flame. From outside she heard footsteps,
someone else who slept little. Keeta opened the lodge mat
to Naana, who waited by a sitting stone. "Shh," admonished
Keeta. "Come inside."

Naana shook her head. She held out a small pouch. "This
is it. Take it to them."

Keeta hesitated.

"Keeta," Naana said in her quiet, nudging way, the way
she'd acquired as a child and had never lost. "This is what
Wautog would have done. "

Keeta took the pouch. Its lumpy contents pushed out the sewn skins.

"You remember what I told you?" Naana asked.

Keeta smiled at that. Naana had repeated her instructions many times, afraid that Keeta wouldn't grasp the importance of the details. Naana smiled in return, quickly, reluctantly, as if her mouth had forgotten how. Then she abruptly turned and slipped back into the gray morning.

Inside, Menuhkeu was awake. He grabbed Keeta's hand as she stepped back inside and brought it in to him, letting her fingers caress his face and his head, rabbit fur framing his chin.

Bi-Bo had arrived, chilled winds that whipped across the water and the marshes, but still the Roanoke trading party moved quickly in four canoes, westward through the sound, toward the river that led to the home of the Choanoak. Keeta was glad that her father, Adchaen, had come along this time, riding in a canoe behind hers. The warriors took care as they moved along Weapemeok lands, as some of the wassadors had made camp on them, staying now for many months.

On the second day, dense, gray-white clouds pushed in from the east, pressing heavily against the sky. Squirrels disappeared into their drays and the birds sat quiet, their heads pulled into their bodies. The Roanoke quickened their pace.

A light snow had begun to fall by the time they reached Choanoak lands, pulled their canoes out of the river, and tied them securely. Along the path, still some distance from the village, they met the first of the Choanoak sentries, seasoned warriors, fully painted. Menatonon was on guard.

Keeta watched how her father greeted the warriors with calm voice and posture. Wampeikuc stood close behind him, his shoulders wide, his legs strong, and his face impassive. She glanced at Menuhkeu. He mirrored his father. Keeta reached up to touch Mishoo, strapped at her back. Someday he would stand with the same strength, she thought, and her heart swelled with an ache of thankfulness for the Creator. The Roanoke were not as many as the Choanoak, but they were no less strong, no less brave.

The snow fell harder as they entered the village. Rather than making their own camp, the party took over a handful of the many lodges that sat empty and unused, after the wassador's invisible poison arrows had come to the Choanoak villages. The lodges were in poor repair but preferable to building quick shelter in the oncoming storm.

By the next day, the sky had cleared to white and snow fell idly. Menuhkeu had left to hunt, and Keeta wasn't long alone when, as she had hoped, a visitor appeared in the yard. Not the same shy girl as last year, but a young imp. She took Keeta's hand and stroked the red marks on her skin, smiling, before she pulled her along through the loose snow.

The snow decorated the lodges with a pretty white cover, but Keeta noticed the many empty homes, how the village had quieted from last year. The girl led her through a tangle of paths to what looked like the same large lodge of many skins Keeta had visited last winter.

A fire burned, but the benches around it were only half-full of women and girls. The shy girl who greeted her last year didn't reappear. The woman with the roped necklaces of Roanoke shells was missing, as was the woman whose wrists were circled in inkings. Keeta didn't ask after them, for it made her heart ache to think of it. The women who remained greeted her and made room for her among them. They served her their stew with berries as they sat, some fixing roof mats and others twisting twine and rope. They asked after her journey and talked of the snow.

One mother took Mishoo into her arms and praised how

he had grown, admiring his fat arms and shiny hair. The Choanoak mother rubbed walnut oil on his skin and sang little songs to him, and Mishoo smiled and grabbed at her nose. Keeta thought of the songs her Mama had sung to Mishoo. She hoped that her son would remember his grandmother's words and the music of her songs.

The soft singing floated underneath the chatter until an old woman, the one they called "oldest relative," began to sing as well, first with the same tune, and then with another. "The Creator," she sang, "has asked me to tell you the story of Mi-she-kae, a story of the first people."

The other women clapped in a soft rhythm in thanks, while the storyteller closed her eyes and looked upward, her chin bobbing gently in time.

"Nanabohzo had been napping when two quarreling blue jays woke him. Cranky and groggy," the storyteller yawned broadly, "he followed the scent of grilling fish to where two brothers sat cooking their catch over a fire." Here she sniffed her nose in an exaggerated manner. "Nanabohzo asked for some and they happily shared a juicy piece. 'Watch out, it's hot!' they warned him, but Nanabohzo grabbed at the fish and burned his hand."

Here the storyteller shook her hand at the wrist and made a face of pain, and one small child mimicked her face, which caused the adults to smile. A small, thin woman came out of the back of the lodge and sat next down Keeta. As the story went on, she ran her crooked finger over the marks on Keeta's arm.

"In pain," the story went on, "Nanabohzo raced to the water to cool his burn. In his hurry, he tripped over a stone and fell on Mi-she-kae the turtle, who was sunning herself on the beach.

'Oh, oh, oh,' cried Mi-she-kae, for at that time she had no hard shell, but was only soft skin and bone. Nanabohzo felt terrible and wondered, what can I do?"

Here, the old woman looked to the children again and asked, "What can Nanabohzo do?"

"Give her a shell!" they chanted. "Give her a shell!"

"And so he did! He put one shell on top and one shell on the bottom, so that Mi-she-kae was in the middle."

The thin woman turned Keeta's arm this way and that, pressing her fingers onto the marks, in a probing, questioning way, then touching the marks on her face. Keeta wondered if the Choanoak women had heard of how she had traveled to the other world, to the entrance of the land of the dead and been sent back to this one. Keeta felt calm with the woman's prodding. Perhaps she was like Wautog, and now Naana as well, practiced in healing.

"The shell is round like Mother Earth," continued the storyteller. "The round hump is like the hills and mountains. The shell is divided into many parts, each different, yet each connected by the Mother. 'When danger threatens,' Nanabohzo told her, 'you can pull your head and your legs in for protection.' Mi-she-kae was very, very pleased, and she listened carefully.

Nanabohzo continued. 'You have four legs, one for each direction—north, south, east, and west. When your legs are drawn in, all directions are lost. Your tail will show the many lands our people have been to, and your head will point in the direction to follow. You will be able to live in the water and carry your house with you at all times.'"

The woman let these words sit before she ended her story. "Mi-she-kae thanked Nanabohzo for this wonderful gift, and she pushed herself along the shore and disappeared into the water. And, ever since that day, turtle has been special to our people and she still proudly wears her two shells."

The woman closed her eyes. In the flickering light of the fire, Keeta looked down at her own changed skin, once smooth and soft, now marked and toughened. Maybe this new shell would offer the protection of Nanabohzo and, like Mi-she-kae, she should be grateful.

She took the root Naana had taken from the swamp, the pitcher plant that had saved her life, out of her pouch. She handed it to the woman sitting next to her, repeating exactly what Naana had taught her—where it had been found, how she had used it, and what had been its effects. The last part was easy. This was the medicine that had brought Keeta back to this world.

Choanoak Territory
Menatonon's Council

On the morning of Menatonon's council, the winter sun shone in a crisp blue sky. The Roanoke warriors woke early to bathe in a swirling pool of the Moratuk River. From the shallow snow clinging to the banks, Menuhkeu stepped out onto a rounded boulder rimmed in ice. He stood and took in the sparkling around him, how the snow and moving water reflected the sunlight and sent it scattering in many directions. Stepping into the swift stream, unfrozen even in winter, he poured the chilled water over his skin. A sharp spasm shot throughout his body, and his mind cleared.

Wanchese, recently bathed, stood near him facing the sun. The spirit traveler breathed deeply, in and out. Turning, he caught Menuhkeu's eye and acknowledged him with a nod.

"Are the streams this refreshing across the sea?" asked Menuhkeu in his easy manner. Menuhkeu caught his father's look of worry at the question. The Roanoke had avoided asking Wanchese direct questions since his return, waiting instead for him to volunteer information.

"Their streams and rivers stink. No one could bathe in them," Wanchese answered.

This was yet one more of Wanchese's statements that the Roanoke couldn't fully comprehend. How could a river stink? Menuhkeu wanted to ask.

"Where do they bathe then?" Menuhkeu asked instead. Wampeikuc and Adchaen slowed as they stepped out of the river, listening.

"They don't bathe. You've smelled them." Wanchese

watched Menuhkeu struggle with the information, his face impassive.

"Yes, I have," agreed Menuhkeu, but still he was confused. "Do their women smell as well?"

Wanchese nodded. "And the children." He clapped Menuhkeu on the shoulder. "Especially the babies," he said, smiling.

The warriors nodded in appreciation, grateful for the joke, mostly glad to see their old friend smile.

The previous year, when Menuhkeu had sat in the great Choanoak council, he could not see beyond the crowds of people circling around. This year, sitting next to Keeta, their sparse numbers allowed for gaps, with views to the lodges, some empty in the distance. How could it be possible that the poison arrows had the power to fell so many? "Do you see the difference?" he whispered to his wife, and she nodded. Among those gathered, Menuhkeu recognized Okisko, the Weapemeok weroance, and various representatives from some of the smaller Secotan villages, their alliance still in disarray. Menuhkeu watched how Menatonon acknowledged each visitor, the lesser and the greater, by looking at their faces and welcoming their presence.

The Choanoak spirit traveler who had greeted the guests in the last trading council was nowhere to be found. Menuhkeu had overheard talk that a poison arrow had killed him. This year the Choanoak spirit guide, his hair crested like a woodpecker's on his bare head, sang a song of welcome. A group assembled from the tribes beat the striking sticks and shook the gourds, and one man, a Weapemeok, played the flute as well, an instrument not often heard by the Roanoke, as it takes many hours to construct and is difficult to play. Its sound was like a bird, but its rhythm was human. Menuhkeu enjoyed how the music joined the two creatures together.

The spirit guide sang of the changes that had come since the wassadors, of the sickness, of the visitors who do not leave. He asked the Creator to guide the people in their choices for the future. He concluded with the song of unity, as Nanabohzo taught:

We are the stars that sing,
We sing with our light.
We are the birds of fire,
We fly over the sky.
Our light is a voice,
We make a road for the spirits,
For the spirits to pass over.
Among us are three hunters who chase a bear.
There never was a time when they were not hunting.
We look down on the mountains,
This is the song of the stars.

After the beating sticks' echoes melted away, the spirit guide lit the pipe and the appowac was passed from one to the next. The talking began. Those gathered attempted to unravel what had happened over the last months. Not every village had seen a wassador, but every village had losses from their invisible poison arrows. Menuhkeu listened to the stories of smaller villages that had lost too many to maintain themselves, and so had been forced to join with neighbors to keep their fields and their temples.

This information brought a somber pause to the gathering. After a few quiet minutes, Menuhkeu saw Menatonon nod at Wingina, who then nodded at Wanchese, seated nearby, black crow feather hanging by his ear.

Wanchese looked up at the many dozens of people sitting around the fire and the many more wandering behind, either serving food or sitting and listening. Menuhkeu looked down at his hands resting on his knees. People of his own village didn't understand a lot of what Wanchese said about his travels, how would this council take his words?

Wanchese began by telling of his trip, of the four kizis he had spent on the wassador ship. Then, he spoke of their land, of how great in number the people and how busy their villages. He described the talking leaves, which held stories of their people. Many of the visitors at the council were confused, and couldn't follow. Menuhkeu knew that Keeta had seen these leaves for herself, as had some of the others gathered. Some sitting around the circle muttered that the wassadors must have done something to Wanchese's dreams to have him speak of such crazy things. When Wanchese held his arms out, his fingers touching as if wrapped around the trunk of a small tree, and told them no trunk grew any bigger than this on their land, a cry of disbelief rose.

But others believed his wassador stories. So much had occurred within the last year that had far surpassed anyone's imagination. Those gathered spoke of the noise sticks, their large canoes, their many objects of metal, their soft clothes, their strange language, their inability to feed themselves, and how they walked through the land without taking notice of it. Menuhkeu listened and the other Roanoke said little. What they alone knew after last year's wassador visit, by this year everyone in the area had learned as well.

After much discussion, Menatonon gathered himself up and the others quieted. "The wassadors ask for two things, again and again. They ask for food, and they ask for copper."

Menatonon waited for this to be discussed and agreed on before he continued. "The men of metal only want more metal. So let us tell them where the copper is to be found."

Menuhkeu and many of those around him were confused. The only metal to be found was the copper that came the west, far away in the mountains, from a people with whom they had no direct contact and who were far more populous than any of the people of the coast. How could they give wassadors metal over which they had no control?

Menatonon continued. The coastal people had no power to give copper to the wassadors. But the wassadors didn't know this. "We," Menatonon explained, "have no fire sticks or poison arrows, but we can use our greater knowledge to our advantage, while being careful to appear to give the wassadors whatever they ask for."

He laid out a plan: they would tell the wassadors the copper was up the Moratuk River. All the people along the river would move inland, so that there would be no one to give them food as they traveled upstream. If the wassadors didn't die of starvation by this point, they would then enter the heart of the Mangoak territory, home to a fierce and unwelcoming people, who would surely kill them.

Menuhkeu felt a rush of excitement at the thought of finally fighting back against those whom he had long regarded as the enemy. He looked to his right and saw in Adchaen's face a desire for action. Wanchese's face mirrored a lust for revenge.

Only Okisko, weroance of the Weapemeok, resisted. The Weapemeok had a large camp of wassadors on their land, and he feared that if the scheme went wrong, his villages would be the first to feel their reprisal. Menuhkeu wondered at this reluctance. Roanoke Island also hosted wassadors, and many Roanoke warriors were more than eager to go into the wassador camp and prove themselves.

It was decided that each leader present would take the plan back to the people to judge its worth. All agreed it made sense to wait until just before the herring returned to execute the plan, for this was the time when food was hardest to come by.

Dasemunkepeuc
Keeta and First Mother Show the Girls How to Count

A corridor of late-spring sky soared above Keeta, First
Mother, and three girls as they took the southwest path
out of the village. After an hour of walking briskly through
budded trees, they veered off to the north and walked more
carefully in denser brush.

"There." First Mother pointed to the large gray boulder,
slightly skimmed with soft green lichen. She walked toward
the pair of white pines that grew pressed against the rock,
their roots twined up the granite sides like a web, and knelt
on the needle-littered ground. The three girls copied, kneeling neatly around First Mother and Keeta in a semicircle.

Keeta felt the warm sun on the backs of her feet and calves.
The burst of warmth after cold made her feel like a girl again,
when she had loved running in the dappled sunlight of the
ancestor trees.

"Here." First Mother handed them each a large clamshell
for digging.

Keeta had shared the stories she had heard at Menatonon's
council, of villages decimated by sickness, the people unable
to carry on their work, and First Mother understood—they
needed to teach all they knew to the girls who were ready to
listen, as soon as possible. And so First Mother and Keeta
had started, a few girls at a time, so that they would feel
special and take their task seriously.

The girls took their shells and dug away the leaves, twigs,
small rocks, and dirt that blocked the entrance to the small
cave to reveal the mats. Lifting them gently to the side, the

entrance appeared. First Mother sent the girls into the hole one by one, to count and to inspect the baskets of food. First Mother and Keeta had stored the provisions late last summer. Both knew exactly what was there.

A gentle breeze rustled a nearby dogwood, and the scent of its flowers wafted about.

Chogen's remaining sister pulled herself up out of the hole after the others. She brushed the dirt off her hands with the fallen needles. "I counted thirty-eight baskets," she announced.

"Twenty filled with corn, sixteen with black walnuts, and two with acorns," added a deer clan girl from the Namohs family, who had lost most of her brothers.

"But," added Wanchese's granddaughter, "two of the corn baskets have been eaten and have large holes in the back, and much of the walnuts are damp and covered in mold."

First Mother nodded. Keeta handed Mishoo to Chogen's little sister and sidled her way into the cave herself, to see how well they had counted.

In the dark space, she made her way along the walls with her hands, counting up and down as she went. Between the corn section and the baskets of nuts, Keeta stopped—there were so many uneaten baskets this year. Her breath shortened as a vacant place opened up inside of her. Her mother, Auwepu... each full basket reflected an empty place at meals.

Keeta felt as if she were standing on the ledge of a high ravine, her toes creeping out over the edge as the emptiness pulled at her, willing her to jump off. How easy it would be to lean in and fall forward and be taken down, down, like a stone racing toward the ground. "Wait," she reminded herself, "I am here to count baskets and not people."

She touched the blue flowers on her medicine bag, drew a deep breath, and continued the count.

Back at the surface, Keeta was met by three serious faces,

each aware of being taught a task above what was expected at her age, and each waiting to see how well she had done. Keeta's instinct leaned toward sharp truth—she wanted to blurt out that they had miscounted, that there were forty-three baskets and twelve of them had large holes. Instead, she shook her head at First Mother, who put her hand gently on the shoulder of the girl closest to her.

"The mold can be boiled away," First Mother said. "I will show you how. Now," she took her counting sticks from the bag tied to her waist, "let's see how long thirty-eight baskets will last. Then, we will go and count again."

Keeta also kept to herself what she had understood while standing in the dark, damp space, surrounded by plenty of food. Clearly, the wassadors had killed the Roanoke people so that they would need less, so they would have extra. Menatonon had been right. To protect themselves, the Roanoke should give the wassadors all they asked for, so that they saw no more need to kill to create a surplus. Then, when they least expected it, the Roanoke would betray them.

Roanoke Island
The Men and Boys Set the Weirs, and Hashap Traps a Wassador

The fish moon rose east over the sound, and red budded on the witch hazel. With nets slipped over lengths of poles, the men and boys from Dasemunkepeuc and Roanoke Island set the weirs in the spring-blue water.

The poles reached through the waves and deep into the sand and were anchored with heavy rocks. The nets, woven throughout the winter, were strung from the poles to make the weirs. Each year, the men chose the place where the herring would give their lives, as well as the place the herring would swim free, in order to leave some to come back the next year.

Menuhkeu and Asku stood with Granganimeo at the mouth of the broad tidal river that ran inland. The chilled water made the weroance's wrists and ankles ache, as the three lodged a long pole in a group of rocks.

Granganimeo nearly didn't survive the winter just passed. Weakened in body by the disease that took almost a quarter of his people, including his wife, Kautantowit, and two of his grandchildren, he was also diminished in spirit by his inability to protect his people from the invaders, the wassadors he had first welcomed, these friends who were not his friends.

The pole set, the men returned to the shore for another. Menuhkeu and Asku greeted Aquandut, who sat untangling nets on the sand. As they talked, Hashap joined them, and the two brothers exchanged glances. Menuhkeu made a move to leave them alone, but Aquandut held up his hand. "You can tell them," he said to Hashap.

"I'll show you," Hashap invited.

The four slipped away from the beach and headed toward what was now the wassador end of the island, a narrow, triangular section of land bordered on two sides by the bay. They hurried along, taking care not to break unnecessary twigs or tamp down the brown grass.

They arrived at a small clearing underneath a broad beech. Hashap pointed to a sprung trap—the noose had been lifted, the prey taken.

"Why are you trapping now?" said Asku, voicing what was also Menuhkeu's question. The Roanoke did not trap when the animals began their nests or raised their young.

"No, you've got it wrong," answered Hashap. "I wasn't after the game. Look." He pointed to a tightened noose and, a few feet away, thick drops of blood spotted on the brown, winter ground. "A squirrel was caught in here, I checked this morning. But I left it there." He stepped toward the blood. "When the squirrel was taken from the trap, it sprung an arrow here," Hashap pointed. "And the arrow found its target."

"What was its target?" asked Asku.

Menuhkeu saw at once. "The wassador who's been stealing from your traps," he said. "The thief was your target."

Hashap nodded. He turned, following the trail of blood, a drop here, a drop a few yards forward, with the others behind, until they reached edge of the wassador camp. A few figures wandered at a distance, but there were no signs of wassadors readying for battle or singing a war song, despite the act of aggression.

They returned to the beach. When they had put distance between themselves and the wassador camp, their pace slowed. A gust of wind shifted the heavy branches of a nearby pine.

"This is a dangerous game," said Asku.

Menuhkeu regarded Aquandut, who had lost his wife and unborn child.

Hashap's words flowed quickly. "Each trace of wassador blood is so little compared to the blood we have lost to their poison arrows. I would have to set as many traps as there were stars in the sky to bring back the balance of things."

Out in the bay came scattered shouts of the Roanoke looping nets onto poles.

"Our people haven't survived since the beginning of the world by being unwilling to adapt to new enemies," commented Menuhkeu.

Aquandut put a hand on his brother's shoulder. "It's more dangerous to do nothing at all."

Dasemunkepeuc
Another Illness Arrives

"It seems the wassadors have sent us more poison arrows,"
Naana explained to Chogen. "This new illness begins with
a small rattle in the chest, coming in the night." They sat
in Wautog's old lodge, where Naana still stored some of the
healing plants. The walls wouldn't last the next winter, but
she hadn't had the chance to move all the supplies to a new
safe spot.

Chogen listened carefully.

"A person goes to sleep in the dark, and when he wakes up
in the sunlight there is a tug in his breathing or his head is
heavy with too much water. The symptoms worsen quickly,
and the sick ones grow hot until they began to cough."

"We will steam thyme or sassafras or boneset," replied the
boy. "If they breathe it in, it will open their breaths."

Naana nodded her agreement. Chogen would have his
moon trek next fall. Naana wondered if she could encourage
him to travel to the mountains to search for plants found
only in the higher place, or if that would interfere with his
warrior passage.

She wondered what she would do without him. Unlike
the first poison arrows, this illness brought familiar symptoms, but she didn't know if her remedies could hold them
back. Bent on taking the very young, the very old, and
those weakened or whose spirit hadn't recovered from the
last sickness, this illness seemed just as dangerous, and she
counted twenty ill within a few days. Naana worried her
supplies wouldn't hold, and that she and Chogen would be

swept into the next world by this new round of sickness, leaving no one to care for the others.

Keeta lay on the rabbit skin blanket and listened to Menuhkeu's breathing—full breaths of air going in, resting a beat, and then flowing out, his chest rising and falling in his sleeping body. Her back against her husband, she took an arm and held it close.

Mishoo's shallow breaths came more quickly. The speed of the breaths in and out reminded Keeta of a hummingbird's rapidly beating wings, her son lightly suspended in the world, like the small bird hovering over a blossom.

The night passed while she lay between the two, enveloped by their warmth. In their breathing lived the Creator, the gentle rocking of the earth—so much that was good that she could not bear to sleep, for fear of what might be taken from her if she were off her guard.

Dasemunkepeuc
The New Illness Opens Keeta's Door and Comes In

Her guard had not been fierce enough. By the following morning, Menuhkeu's breath rattled as he exhaled, Mishoo's skin was hot to the touch, and Keeta's chest felt heavy, as if a log sat on it. Keeta made bark tea, and they lay on their rabbit blanket, letting the sickness take its course.

This is the story Keeta told.

Mishoo did not have the strength to wait it out. At the very end of their son's illness, Keeta and Menuhkeu watched as, like soft down, tiny feathers sprouted on the baby's skin. Airy growths that shifted with the slightest of movement in the air, they multiplied quickly. They appeared first on his head, and then next on his back, around the curve of his thick buttocks and thighs. Soon, only the round circle of his face—the eyes, the nose, the mouth, a bit of cheek—remained free of the soft fuzz anchored deeply in.

The parents sent for Naana, who came at once with her deerskin bags of carefully gathered medicine, only the best for the precious son of her dear friend. Arriving as the sun was setting, she pulled back the flaps to enter the lodge and sent an orange beam of sunlight across the floor onto the child, a path Naana knew, to the land of the dead. Keeta and Menuhkeu, dizzy with their own fevers, lay on each side of the baby cradled in a willow bed lined with a thick rabbit skin.

On his head, the light down had grown to tufts of golden brown. Naana gently turned the child over and traced her finger over the delicate feathers on the back, an inch or so in length, colored in grays, tans, browns, and the occasional white and black, especially under his chin. As she lay him back down, she noticed a gleam of yellow in his eyes. It wouldn't be long now.

The healer boiled some roots and leaves in a small pot she carried with her. When they had cooled, she handed a gourd full to Menuhkeu, who had kept his eyes open. He drank the whole portion while Naana sat next to him.

She let the medicine do its work and, after a bit, he sat up. Bending over the cradle, he lifted his son into his arms. With two fingers, he stroked the small section of his face still clear, just under his eyes and above his nose, grown increasingly sharp.

Menuhkeu hadn't gotten the spotted disease, but Naana saw how the years had gathered to him anyway, thinness in his face, sadness in his eyes. He replaced his son in his cradle and looked to Naana.

She nodded her head. Together they lifted Keeta up into a sitting position, and cradled her into Menuhkeu's lap as Naana worked her fingers into Keeta's mouth to encourage her to sip and swallow the medicine. It took a long while. When the gourd was empty, they lay her back down on the bed, and Naana took her leave into the evening.

Menuhkeu lay down next to his wife and held their child close to his chest, so he could not leave them. The three slept together in their fever throughout the night. But their efforts were to no avail. In the night, Mishontoowau flew away, leaving behind only a packet of bones to bury with his ancestors.

That is the story Keeta told, for the truth of it was too hard to bear—that the wassadors had sent a poison arrow with Mishoo's name on it.

Roanoke Island
Lane Demands Punishment from Granganimeo

The wassador Lane never asked a visitor to sit or to smoke. Granganimeo suspected that if their spirit traveler, Harriot, didn't intervene, their every meeting would be conducted standing, and the Roanoke would be like the deer in the wood, their ears always pricking, sensing danger, their minds never still to consider and think.

Yesterday, Harriot had walked into his village to request yet another meeting with the weroance Lane. Now Harriot stood before him, with his Roanoke greetings, gesturing them into the wassador lodge. And, according to Manteo, the message was so important that the wassadors had waited for the translator to arrive from Croatoan to deliver it.

"He invites us to enter," said Manteo, aside.

Granganimeo barely nodded in response. He had visited this dank and dreary lodge many times throughout the winter. Each time he was met with a request for corn, for squash, for meat, for beans and now, most likely, for the fish that swam into the weirs spaced out along the sound. He didn't need the spirit traveler to explain this request to him. He knew it too well already.

The smell of the unbathed wassadors met Granganimeo at the entrance and, not for the first time, he wondered if this was another one of their tricks, a way of distracting their enemies, like a skunk. Granganimeo stood, as there was no mat, Manteo next to him. Aquandut stayed by the door, his back against the wall, ready to alert the other Roanoke stationed at the edge of the wassador village if need be. He made himself as small as possible so that the wassadors would feel no threat and the part of their minds that worried would forget that he was there at all.

Lane spoke. His bulk had diminished in the long winter months, but the force of his anger and command still simmered. His presence was, as ever, unpleasant.

"He is very angry," said Manteo. "He says we have done him a great injury, for which we must be punished."

Granganimeo waited.

Harriot spoke and then clapped his hands together. A wassador left the lodge, leaving one wassador standing guard behind Lane. Only a shout and the light whistling of the wind blowing through the cracks in the walls disturbed the silence. A few minutes later, the wassador returned with a large, heavy bundle of white, soft cloth. He placed the bundle gently at Lane's feet.

Lane knelt, and such a softness came onto his face that Granganimeo wildly worried for an instant that there was a child wrapped within.

The wassador unwound the cloth to reveal a dead animal. The carcass resembled one of the wassadors' wolf-like creatures kept tied around the camp, creatures that often barked for hours. It had been pierced through the head.

Were they going to eat this now? wondered Granganimeo.

Outside came the sound of chopping.

"What has this to do with us?" said Granganimeo to Manteo, who repeated the question in wassador words.

Harriot reached into a leather bag and pulled out an arrow, which Aquandut recognized as his brother's.

Granganimeo, then Manteo, inspected the arrow before they handed it back to Harriot.

At this, Aquandut shifted his weight.

Granganimeo spoke in low tones to Aquandut, without turning his head, "Tell me."

"You know the wassadors have been stealing from my brother's traps." He paused. "So he set a trap of his own."

Manteo made no sign that he had overheard their conversation, but Granganimeo knew that he must have. He felt acutely the power Manteo had in being the only one of them who knew all the words spoken. How long would it be before he betrayed one side or the other?

"This is not a hunting arrow," Granganimeo lied to Harriot, using his hands to indicate a bow and arrow, and then a snare. "This is a trapping arrow. Only those who touch the trap get this arrow."

Manteo spoke in the wassador tongue.

The wassadors spoke amongst themselves, Lane's words louder than the others, his face tight and impatient. Finally, Harriot spoke. His words were so mangled that Manteo translated.

"The weroance Lane has lost a valuable animal. He says that the man who did this must be brought to him for punishment, that their god would be angry that such damage went unpunished."

Granganimeo felt a burst of fire explode in his chest, and it took all his years of experience to keep quiet. His heart was full of his lost wife, his lost grandchildren, his lost people, and the people who lay now unwell in their lodges with a new disease. A trap set at this time of year would be a warning to everyone except a wassador. Granganimeo had no response.

He turned and left. Manteo spoke smoothly to Lane and Harriot. Most likely promising them all the fish in the weirs, thought Granganimeo, with bitterness.

Later in the day, as Granganimeo sat around the fire and breathed in the delicious scents of cooking fish, he wondered at the heaviness in his head, the small catch in his breathing. He attributed the feeling to sorrow and said nothing to his daughters.

The small heaviness in his lungs increased in the night. When he woke to the sun, there was a certain tug in his chest and his head was overfull of water.

As these were ailments for which there were many various remedies, the family placed a gourd of dried thyme and sassafras in boiled water, while Granganimeo's daughter held his head in the medicated steam.

When the fever came, they applied pine poultices. But then the cough arrived, rattling deep in his chest and making a sound like rocks on the beach of a receding tide.

Dasemunkepeuc
News from Roanoke Island

Menuhkeu caught a flash of blue wings, a bluebird couple
building a nest of pine needles and grasses above. The color
was a burst of cheer. And a welcome diversion, for he had a
bad feeling about the canoe making its way across the choppy
bay from Roanoke Island. A lone crow circled over the canoe,
like a warning that those paddling were carrying bad news.

Late afternoon, the sun's slanted rays glanced golden off the
waves, obscuring the identity of the canoe's passengers until
they were close to the shore. Then Aquandut and Manteo
greeted him, their faces grim. "We have something for our
weroance Wingina," said Manteo briefly, as they pulled the
canoe to the high water line.

Menuhkeu nodded. The crow still circled above, black
wings slicing the sky, and the three headed toward the village.

They found Wingina outside his lodge, on a sitting stone.
Aquandut said nothing and kept his eyes lowered as he handed Wingina the deerskin packet he had crossed the sound to
deliver. Wingina took it. He slowly untied the grass knots.
Out came his cousin's six copper bracelets. Granganimeo
was dead.

Wingina dropped the bracelets to the ground and let out
a long wail. The sound from his throat pierced Menuhkeu's
spirit to the core—Wingina's pain was his pain. Wingina's
rage was his rage.

Alerted by the sound, many in the village ran toward
their weroance. After his keening, Wingina turned and left.
Menuhkeu, fighting off the lingering weakness of his sickness,

chased after him, many in the village following.

They raced down the path to the river, underneath the canopy of green pods of leaves, ready to burst. At water's edge, Wingina raised his arms to the sky, head back and eyes closed. The crowd that had followed him grew. Lowering his hands, he stripped himself, and plunged into the river rushing down from the mountains.

To Menuhkeu, it seemed his weroance would never emerge. Then Wingina burst to the surface. His face and shoulders rose above the clear, moving water. His body reflected both the sun from above and the brown stones below in a prism of energy. Menuhkeu drank in this energy, like the thirsty person he was.

Wingina made his way back to shore. He stood in the sun, and his strength coursed through them all.

Dasemunkepeuc
Wingina's Decision

Wingina called a council.

Manteo, charged with passing on Lane's message, waited until the outpouring of grief had passed and the village had gathered at the meeting circle before sharing Lane's demand.

"What was this animal to them?" questioned Asku as those gathered tried to make sense of the source of Lane's injury. Most of the warriors had by now seen the wolf-like creatures, called dogs, tied by ropes in Lane's village.

"They must be sacred animals," answered Aquandut, remembering Lane's face as he unwrapped the dead creature. "They don't eat them. They feed them."

"We have to give them what they want," entreated Ensenore. "Who knows what else they can do to us?"

"We give them what they want and still we are dying," replied Wingina. "It is time to act on Menatonon's plan."

"He's right," said Wampeikuc. Murmurs of assent passed through the group.

"How do we know the Weapemeok won't betray us?" Ensenore asked. "A group of wassadors have lodged in their territory for most of the winter. How do we know that Okisko and the Weapemeok don't just pretend to admire Menatonon's plan, so that they can then take our fishing and shellfish territories?"

"And what good are our fishing and shellfish if we have no people left?" answered Menuhkeu, aware that his voice was tinged with anger.

"Menatonon's plan is a sound one," said Aquandut. "And

we are running out of choices." Ensenore folded his arms and said nothing, but the majority nodded and affirmed Aquandut's words.

Wingina, his face like stone, looked around the circle before he turned to Manteo. "Tell Lane that we accept our punishment," he said. "Tell them their greatness must come from the Creator, and that we have only to learn from their superior ways. Tell them they are invited to visit Menatonon and that he promises to give them access to his copper. And, as a token of friendship, we will set up a weir for them near their encampment."

"Lane will be very pleased," Manteo answered.

Menuhkeu watched Manteo carefully as spoke. The pain on the young spirit traveler's face, though, reflected the pain of those seated around him.

Menuhkeu reported to Wingina after a visit to Roanoke Island that, from all appearances, Lane had taken the Roanoke bait. Within days, the wassador's largest canoe returned from Weapemeok territory. Then, smaller canoes ferried items from the wassador camp to this larger canoe for the better part of a day. The wassadors moved their dogs, the squat creatures with mouths of sharp teeth they kept on chains, onto the ships as well.

The next morning, this large canoe headed west into the sound. Wingina sent Asku north to trail Lane and the wassadors as they visited Menatonon and the Choanoak, and then, perhaps, to Mangoak territory.

Back at the wassador camp, Lane had left only a few dozen men, at most.

Dasemunkepeuc
Keeta and Naana Share Some Things and Keep Some Secrets

Throughout the day, Mishoo's absence could be more easily accounted for. Maybe he was visiting with cousins, or
perhaps his grandfather had taken him down to the water
to bathe. Yet when Keeta entered her lodge, his fur-covered
cradle lay empty and the air above it hung chilly without
his deep sleeping breaths.

Still, in a village replete with loss, the pleasant smell of
cooking herring over low fires wafted. Keeta sat by her yard
fire, repairing a herring rack to cook fish for Wequassus and
Minneash, who lay sick with fever, coughing in their lodge.

Naana appeared carrying empty gourds. Keeta looked
up. Her friend looked tired, her eyes were hollow, but she
carried the warmth of the Creator in her, and this piqued
Keeta's heart with an ache, although she couldn't say why.

"You've taken a long route to the water," Keeta commented.

The quiet of the yard, without Mishoo's usual chatter and
the fuss around him, sat heavily. Even the robins chose to
roost on a tree at a distance away.

Naana put down her gourds and sat.

"Is First Mother still coughing?" Keeta asked.

Naana nodded. She reached for Keeta's hands, pulling her
fingers away from the broken herring rack. She took them
in her own and rubbed them.

"Mama visits me often," said Keeta after they had sat like
that for some time. "She curls herself around me when I
sleep."

Naana nodded. "Auwepu visits me as well."

Keeta recalled the leaves the wassador White had made, the images of the messenger boy, Mese, and of Auwepu, with child. Those images had given her an uneasy feeling, and both Mese and Auwepu had been killed in the first round of poison arrows. Keeta hesitated. It didn't seem right to discuss these things with Naana.

The sounds of the running feet of small children gently padded the path behind the lodge. A young girl laughed.

Keeta thought of how she woke each morning with empty arms. The absence of her son's weight gave her a frightening lightness. "But…Mishoo…he never comes."

Naana considered Keeta, her voice so quiet, her eyes without their usual glitter of fire and knowing. Naana thought on what she had seen in her work with the sick and the dying. The small lives that left like a puff of wind. This was not knowledge to share with anyone not a healer. Naana took a root out of her carrying bag. "Here," she said to Keeta. "Chew on this."

"It's not necessary," protested Keeta.

"It's spring," replied Naana. "The herring run. It's better if our blood runs inside us as like a river as well."

Keeta took the root Naana had given her and chewed it until the mash in her mouth disappeared. She pulled the remaining tiny strings from her teeth and left them on the ground.

A little revived, she stood and followed the path through the cedars. The ancestor trees threw patterns of shadow into the bright, spring light. At first, Keeta's head was empty and her limbs weak and she felt she could hardly take a step, but little by little she began to notice things—the soft, flat leaves on the ground, the twitters of the squirrels, the knocking of the woodpecker, the hoo-hoo-hoo of the mourning dove.

Arriving at the beach, she saw men and boys standing in

ripples of water, adjusting a weir, carrying a basket, or lifting heavy rocks to secure the poles. Further out, the sun lit the waves. Closer to shore, the clear water pulled over the sand, dragging a little kelp.

She watched Menuhkeu as he bent over to lay a heavy basket of fish on the sand. A shudder went through her, like the beginning of tears, but also like the return of feeling.

Dasemunkepeuc
Asku Returns with News

Menuhkeu heard the news first as he was returning from the lodge of the dead with Chepeck. The two had spent the morning singing Menuhkeu's mother to the next world.

"I have seen it," Asku told them. "Lane is headed up the Moratuk River in search of copper. The Choanoak along the river have fled inland, so the wassadors will meet no help along the way."

Chepeck lifted his hands to the sky, "Thank you to the Creator for this!" he said, aloud. He adjusted his rabbit skin cloak. "Thank you to the Creator for this!" he repeated more softly, to himself.

Menuhkeu breathed deeply. He felt the same relief, but the sadness at what he had lost threatened to overwhelm him. He needed to see Keeta. He excused himself from the healer and, rather than heading to the meeting ground or Wingina's lodge where there surely would be discussion about this latest event, he headed back to their lodge.

Dasemunkepeuc
Owush Pays a Visit

A waning crescent slit the dark sky low in the west, and the stirrings of the village quieted under the bright stars. Keeta sat over a low fire, heating bark tea for Minneash who, still coughing, had moved in and out of fever for almost two weeks. Menuhkeu sat next to her. She felt the warmth of his thigh against hers, his arm across her shoulder. Her father rested on a sitting stone across from them. Adchaen had moved into their lodge when her Mama had died, one of many changes taking place all over the village as families reordered themselves.

"So Menatonon has not betrayed us," said Keeta, going over Asku's news. "And the Weapemeok?"

"Perhaps when they saw that the wassadors really could be lured up the river, they saw the wisdom of the plan," answered Menuhkeu.

"Or Menatonon and the Choanoak warriors convinced them to go along," added Adchaen.

Keeta took the gourd off the fire to cool "So maybe the wassadors won't be back."

"How could Lane survive without food or help? They haven't managed to support themselves for one day since they've arrived," said Menuhkeu.

Adchaen laughed grimly. "Except they're still here."

The twittering of a loud squirrel caught their attention. Keeta was on guard, for squirrels are asleep in their drays at such an hour, but Menuhkeu smiled at the approach of his brother, Owush. It was an old signal they had used as boys, when their weasel clan games went on for most of a day. He rose to greet him.

"Oh, good, you're here," said Keeta, rising, thinking he had come for tea for Minneash.

"Daughter," said Adchaen, quietly.

His tone chilled her. She looked up as Owush stepped into the low light. He held a bundle.

Nodding briefly at their greeting, he faced Keeta.

Her breath stopped thick in her mouth. She knew at once that Minneash was dead, and what Owush had come for. Keeta looked at her husband in a moment of uncertainty but, standing, Menuhkeu's face rose above the fire and she could not read its features. Owush knelt at her feet and looked up at her. In his eyes she saw a man who had lost his wife, his mother, two sisters, and a niece, all the girls in the family. She saw sorrow and she saw trust. She also saw necessity. She let him put the bundle in her arms.

Peeling away the deerskin, there he was, Pishpesh, looking as Mishoo would look, the sturdy arms and strong legs limp and pressed against his body in the deep and powerful sleep of a child.

She brushed her hand over his thick hair. Of course, we will take him.

She looked up from the baby to her brother-in-law, who remained kneeling before her. "We will care for him as if he were our own, because he is our own."

Owush nodded. He rose and left the lodge, quickly disappearing into the darkness.

That night, as they slept, Keeta felt a break in her heart, a piercing pain that rose through her chest and out her mouth, followed by a fullness that felt almost like exhaustion. This flowed throughout her body, and sleep took her into its arms and wrapped her in its warmest blanket.

Roanoke Island
Keeta Visits Nippe

Without wind, the currents lay flat across the sound. Each dip of the paddle broke thin clouds in a blue sky, reflected in the smooth surface of the water. When Keeta drew the paddle forward, a line of droplets fell, like string of pearls, disappearing into blue. At the age where he could hardly be contained in a pack, Pishpesh laughed and leapt at the sparkling water.

With First Mother ill with the cough, Keeta made the trip alone. So many of the Roanoke Island families had moved back to Dasemunkepeuc that First Mother and Keeta worried about the crops on the island. They wondered whether it made sense to plant on Roanoke Island at all. They also wondered whether, with all the sickness, some corn or beans had been stashed somewhere in the fall and then forgotten by spring.

After pulling the canoe on the beach, and knowing that Granganimeo's family was in tatters, Keeta went to the shell polishers and to Aquandut, a friend to her husband and a member of the powerful bear clan family. And, she couldn't forget, once Auwepu's husband. Aquandut led her to Nippe, the girl who was once a Weapemeok.

They found her kneeling in the turned-over soil, several girls grouped around her, baskets of seeds by their side.

Nippe stood and greeted Keeta with the respect due a First Mother. Keeta surprised herself by the ease with which she accepted the girl's deference. "I am teaching the girls to plant," Nippe explained. "And, "she added shyly, "I'm using some Weapemeok lessons."

Remembering lessons learned from her Choanoak visits, something in the girl's manner sparked Keeta's curiosity. "I would like to learn as well," Keeta answered. "Let me listen in."

Nippe returned to the dirt. "Draw the circle of the sun," she instructed the girls.

They smiled shyly. They didn't know what she meant.

News of Keeta's visit quickly spread through the small village, and soon other Roanoke women came and greeted Keeta with respect as well, as they gathered to listen.

"This I learned from my grandmother," Nippe explained, with a smile. Drawing a circle, she marked the east where the sun began its loop around the sky, and then the west, where the sun set. "Once the circle is marked, place the beans and squash always on the southwest side."

The women praised her cleverness. One explained, "We plant according to the horizon, for we have always planted on the island."

Keeta nodded in agreement. This new lesson was not based on living with the sea always to the east, but on the sun and so superior because it could be used in different locations.

The girls drew their own circles, dragging their toes through the dirt, and the older women practiced the new trick as well. Keeta set Pishpesh down, and one of the girls gave the baby a small stick so he could feel included.

Keeta learned that young girls, who during last summer's crop would have watched or helped in small ways, would this spring tend mounds on their own. "Are you able to plant as much as last year?" she asked.

The group murmured amongst themselves before Aquandut's sister answered. "We struggle to plant the early corn, to dig over the dirt, to put up the new mounds for the seeds, to pack them in with fish and shells. All this as some still lie in their lodges, weak and coughing."

She paused before continuing. "We plan to plant the same amount as the year before, because the land is already well cleared and we have the seed. "

"And since the wassadors haven't returned to the island in a moon's worth of days, we hope that what we plant will be our own," added Nippe.

"Many families have already joined us at Dasemunkepeuc," said Keeta. "Perhaps you will follow?"

Keeta had expected this idea to be met with much resistance, so she was surprised when the women around her nodded, or said nothing. She had seen the empty lodges, the roof mats falling to the side, the places where the small animals had nibbled at the edges of once well-kept walls.

"Yes, we have discussed that," said Aquandut's sister. "We thank you for coming to remind us that we're welcome."

Keeta replied as she knew First Mother would. "We would be strengthened by your presence."

When the sun stretched their shadows thin, the woman and girls packed up their baskets and diggers and bags of extra seeds, and headed back toward the village. The path home took the western route, with views to the sound and the mainland.

And there, in the glint of the fading sun on the water, came two ships—masts dark, sails full of the warm air that blew from the mainland. The wassadors had returned.

The lightness of their laughter and planting lesson vanished. Keeta felt her stomach tighten and her shoulders hunch up as if against the cold. She saw her own dread reflected on the faces around her as every little girl reached up to take a hand and every woman's pace quickened toward the village. Reaching the village, she motioned for the group to gather once more. "Ready yourselves to leave quickly," she told them. "And when you go, empty your caches, pull them out of the ground—don't leave a seed behind."

Nippe took Keeta's hand. "Auwepu told me many wonderful stories of your village," she said. "I would be honored to visit there."

The tide was with Keeta on her paddle home, a fortunate thing, for the wind had picked up and gray clouds like slate moved across the sky from the northeast. Even though the wassador camp wasn't in view on her route back to Dasemunkepeuc, every bit of the way she felt the wassadors at her back. Even Pishpesh sat quietly in his pack.

Dasemunkepeuc
The Wassadors Return

Keeta pulled her canoe onto the sands of Dasemunkepeuc
and returned to a village in turmoil over the wassador's return. Children had been called in and work put aside as the
Roanoke wrestled with the new reality.

Who were they that they traveled up the Moratuk River
to Mangoak territory and returned? Had they come from
another world? Were they unrecognized ancestors? Keeta
went first to her lodge, which was empty, and then to the
meeting ground, swirling with a crowd of people. A rumor
flew that Manteo had gone with the wassadors and was arriving to explain all. This Keeta dismissed until she saw the
spirit traveler, black crow feather in his hair and wearing his
wassador pants, stride toward the council circle, Wingina,
Wampeikuc, and Wanchese at his side. The crowd silenced
as the four sat. Chepeck and Ensenore arrived, and then
her father stood at her back with a hand on her shoulder.

"Take your place at the circle," he said. "First Mother has
gone to the land of the dead, and Wingina requests it."

Keeta placed her hand over her father's and nodded before
she walked and took a place near the healer. The loss of First
Mother fell on her like a stone, but as the heaviness entered
her, Keeta found the weight a source of strength. A strong
sense of First Mother—her rectitude, her knowledge, her
patience, even the weirs that ringed her thighs—came to
Keeta and she understood these qualities as a part of herself
now. This she knew was blessing.

Chepeck lit a fire, threw on the appowac, and sang of

thanks. When the song was over, Wingina asked Manteo the question every Roanoke wanted to know—how had these wassadors, with no ability to discern edible greens or come across fields with grown crops, with the game driven away and the weirs pulled out of the water along their route, with the villages along the river emptied so that no possibility of resupply appeared, how had they gone up to the river toward the most vicious enemy in the area and returned?

"They must be from another world!" exclaimed Ensenore.

"Their survival wasn't a matter of powers from another world," Manteo responded. "They're human and they need nourishment, like we do."

"Then how did they survive?" asked Wampeikuc.

"It was simple," Manteo replied. "They ate their dogs." The crowd murmured. Keeta hadn't seen these animals, although she, like everyone, had heard the stories of the wolf-like animals, fed and kept on ropes.

Manteo looked slowly around at the people gathered, meeting each one's gaze before he moved on to the next. "You complain they can't hunt, yet they are still here," he said, his voice rising. "You complain they can't fish, yet they are still here. You complain they can't plant, yet they are still here. You complain they can't forage. Yet they are still here."

Then Manteo, for the first time since his return, publicly addressed Wanchese. "You have seen their numbers, my brother."

The council fell silent. Wanchese's opinion had been discredited by some for his wild stories, but his loyalty was never in question. Keeta turned with the others to watch Wanchese's face. It was immobile.

"Answer this, my brother. If all of them, with their numbers, came here," Manteo continued, "would we have any chance against them?"

Keeta held her breath, as if Wanchese's answer would

somehow lead her and all those gathered to some kind of understanding, some kind of solution.

"If all the wassadors that I have seen there?" answered Wanchese. "If they all came here?"

"Yes."

Wanchese's face broke into many pieces, before he readjusted himself to answer the question. But by then, Keeta and all those around her had their answer. "Their numbers are vast," admitted Wanchese. "Their power immense."

At Wanchese's words, Keeta felt as if the breath were taken out of her body, leaving her weak and confused. They had suffered hardship at the hands of the wassadors, but it was the unknown and the disorder that was the hardest to fight. Keeta turned to Wingina as he spoke.

"All we know for certain," said Wingina, and Keeta understood then that a leader's primary job is to make clear the situation so that the people can see to act. "All we know for certain is that these wassadors are our mortal enemies."

Dasemunkepeuc
A Storm Approaches

The morning after the wassadors returned from the north, Keeta and Menuhkeu woke to a low, gray-brown sky. The air hung moist and the new green leaves whispered in the trees. "This doesn't look like a good day to put in seeds," said Keeta to the women who gathered at the meeting ground. "A storm may come and undo all our work." They agreed to hold off on the planting.

As the day went on, animals passed along signs of the coming weather to the Roanoke. On his way to the lodge of the dead, the healer Chepeck noticed the song sparrows were silent. Searching for them in the brush near the river, he found they had left, a strange event. Usually he enjoyed their lilting voices until the locust tree was past bloom.

At the bay, Menuhkeu watched clusters of shad dart about in a frenzy of eating.

Naana, picking mustard plant shoots, saw that the ants had covered the hole to their lodge.

By midday, the wind picking up and the gulls flying inland, the Roanoke pulled the weirs in from the bay. A bad storm with high waves would make a tangle of the nets and send the poles drifting out to sea.

Leaving the holding stones, one by one the men and boys pulled up the poles, laying them across the bottoms of their canoes. They placed the folded nets over the poles, going in this manner from canoe to canoe. When they were finished, they pulled their canoes far into the ancestor trees, fastening them there on long ropes.

The morning's high tide, a moon tide, had traveled so far up the beach it lapped the ancestor trees. Water seeped through the marsh and toward the village, pushed onward by the increasing wind. After the weirs had been pulled, those on Roanoke Island stepped into their canoes and paddled over to Dasemunkepeuc through choppy surf, to lodge through the weather with families at the main village. Keeta and Menuhkeu welcomed many from Aquandut's family, including Nippe, who was quick to tell Keeta that the island women had brought all their seeds with them.

In the late afternoon, Menuhkeu and Keeta hurried to the meeting ground to join the others in deciding what to do. Standing in the rising wind, the tribe discussed the situation. Most wanted to flee inland, away from the storm and away from the wassadors.

All agreed that the coming storm would be large. "We will head for the safety of the valleys," announced Wingina. The valleys were inland, a safe spot shown to them by the ancestors, where the water wouldn't reach them and where they would have some shelter from great wind.

"It's growing dark," pointed out Wanchese. "We won't reach the valleys in time."

"We'll have to go through the marsh," answered Wampeikuc. "It's much quicker that way, a quarter of the time."

"The tide is rising. We won't make it through the marsh now," answered Wanchese.

Wampeikuc nodded in agreement. "The next low tide will be just before dawn. We can wait and move then. We won't be caught near falling trees, and we can see our way."

"Take your seeds," reminded Keeta. "Clean out your caches. Don't leave anything behind for the wassadors or the water."

During the night, the rain began. Keeta listened to the soft plops of single raindrops landing on the roof mats. They soon fell faster and faster, until she could no longer distinguish one from another. Restless, she whispered to Menuhkeu, "Who has the hatchets? We can't leave those behind."

He pulled her close. "My father and Aquandut have the hatchets. You have to sleep. A good warrior sleeps deeply before a battle."

Eventually the shifts and turns of Roanoke Island visitors sleeping in their lodge quieted, and Keeta drifted into sleep.

Keeta woke to a sound she had never heard before, a loud crack, like sharp, quick thunder that broke the silence of the early dawn. In the next instant, she heard shouting, frenzied calls that entered the lodge and spurred those inside to action—Menuhkeu and Aquandut and his brother Hashap to their bows and arrows and clubs and then out the door, Keeta to Pishpesh and her seeds. Nippe grabbed a bag of meal, ready to flee inland.

Fleeing bodies scudded around Keeta like clouds in the faint light as they ran as quickly as they could, carrying children and a few provisions. The women and children are always the prizes of a raid, so within minutes they had left their lodges and headed inland toward the marsh.

"Go with the others," she urged Nippe, but the girl wouldn't leave her side and so, with no time to argue, the two made a quick tour of the village, the shouts of the men moving toward the beach.

Finding no stragglers, Keeta made sure Pishpesh held tight to her, his legs wrapped around her waist, his arms over her shoulders, and she and Nippe ran to catch up to the group.

She put Nippe at the rear so that no one was left behind and moved to the front of the group. Dawn broke gray. The sky was angry. Twists of black clouds sent large gourd-fulls of rain, falling in clumps to the ground, splattering the earth like rocks dropping in a pool.

The tide heading out normally left a dry path inland through the salty marshes. This morning, however, water continued to lap forward. Women had to carry small children on their shoulders through waist-deep pools of moving water, water that grew deeper rather than receding.

The hillock where Keeta and Menuhkeu had spent many pleasant hours had almost disappeared, recognizable only by the tip of the lone bush in the center.

Half-way across the wetland, full daylight made its weak appearance, and Keeta, looking toward the east, saw water creeping steadily toward them, covering the grasses, flattening the horizon, as the sea made its inexorable approach. They traveled on a part of the earth that was half water and half land, on the margins of each. At any point their path could disappear. Keeta urged her companions on, although they needed little urging.

By the time they reached the other side of the marsh, the wind had turned sideward and Keeta clutched Pishpesh to her front, keeping his head out of the driving rain. The wind began to wail, and then to scream so loudly that speech became lost in the noise. It whipped new green leaves off the trees and sent small objects hurtling.

They found the deep ravine, narrow, angled north to south, the long passage that offered protection from the wind and the water. The women worked quickly, gathering brush and sticks to lay across the top, to provide somewhat of a roof.

They didn't talk about what they would do if they were the only remaining women or what could have happened to the men. They said their thanks to the Creator, and waited.

Menuhkeu woke in an instant, his bow and arrows in hand and ready to fly before he left his lodge. Racing toward the sounds of shouting but careful not to expose himself to the unknown, he used the trees and lodges to advance, Aquandut close behind.

After the first crack from what sounded like a wassador weapon, there were two additional cracks, much shouting and sounds of branches breaking. In the dim light, Menuhkeu discerned some motion, and then he heard an additional crack. Someone or something fell some feet ahead of him. A second figure moved in, bent over the fallen figure, and then fled toward the sea. Aquandut chased after the retreating figure, while Menuhkeu went toward the fallen one.

At the moment the Menuhkeu reached the fallen figure, the sun seeped over the horizon. The gray light revealed, splayed on the pine needles, a body, a body without a head. Menuhkeu moved in closer, and he cried out—the long, spindly legs, the four-arrowed inkings with a circle, the arrows with the egret feathers. It was Wingina. Blood pooled out of his neck. Menuhkeu stood up. So shocking was this image, he felt only numb.

Following Aquandut, Menuhkeu raced back through the empty village, toward the beach. The rain picked up and the wind began to speak. Through the ancestor trees he sped, all creatures in hiding from the storm, until he came to a crowd of warriors gathered at the edge of the grasses near the beach, staring out toward the sound. When he reached the group, he saw it as well—two freshly arrived wassador ships rocking in the harbor, with two small wassador canoes paddling rapidly away from the shore.

Asku said to his friend. "They must have come in during the night."

"Wingina is dead," said Menuhkeu. "They stole his head from his neck."

The warriors turned to Menuhkeu.

"What? What did you say?" asked his father, his voice rising.

"They killed him with their weapon and then they took his head from his neck."

"Who would take such a thing?" asked Owush.

"They will take anything," said Wanchese. "They will take everything."

The Roanoke wrapped the weroance Wingina in a deerskin blanket and carried him inland to join the rest of their tribe at the inland shelter.

The storm blew fiercely and the rain came down like a waterfall. When the Roanoke returned to Dasemunkepeuc, three days later, the wassadors ships and canoes were all gone. On Roanoke Island they found Wingina's head, which they took home and wrapped with his body. They also found three wassadors, whom they killed, leaving the carcasses for the animals.

Dasemunkepeuc
One Year Later

Keeta stood on the beach, waiting for the others. Her calves bore the marks of an even net, like the diamonds in a weir, widening gracefully up to her thighs. A short distance away, Pishpesh threw rocks into the water with the vigor of a boy who had seen more than his two summers. The summer wind set the grasses dancing, but Keeta's eyes were drawn out to where the bay met the sea. There, in the narrow passage of churning water between the barrier islands, a wassador ship tossed and turned in its attempt to enter the bay, the first ship sighted since the wassadors fled in the storm late last spring.

She narrowed her eyes with resolve. The marks on her skin, from the first set of poison arrows, had darkened into a mottled pattern that resembled the marks of a turtle shell. Many times over the past winter, Keeta had looked at her skin and drawn courage from its kinship with the sacred turtle. How else would she have been able to rally the women to plant just after the storm, just after Wingina's profane death? How else would she have helped to bring together the Roanoke Island women with those of Dasemunkepeuc? How else would a new life be growing inside her?

Where before she questioned and wondered, now Keeta acted with a clarity and force she had not possessed before she had been marked. She was First Mother of the Roanoke now, and she gathered the role to her, as its responsibilities and duties fortified her.

Menuhkeu came through the path. Pishpesh saw him first,

and the boy struggled out of the shallows, thick legs working hard, to reach his father. Menuhkeu moved to meet the toddler on the sand, but Wampeikuc reached out his hand. "Let the boy struggle," he advised.

Wanchese and the weroance Aquandut quickly followed.

"There," Keeta pointed, when they arrived. "We hear it is only one this time."

The warriors nodded their agreement. Without doubt it was a familiar wassador ship.

They would of course call a council, but the talk would be brief. This time, the Roanoke would not hesitate. This time, the Roanoke knew what they had to do.

Author's Note

Some will rightfully find it untenable that I have chosen to tell this story at all from a point of view I was not born into—Europeans unleashed on the Native People an ethnic cleansing the extent of which Americans have still not owned. And, it's not as if the vibrant and multifaceted culture that is modern Native People haven't told their own stories, many times and in many ways.

When I started, I meant to write this "Mystery of the Roanoke Colony" story from both the settler and the Native People points of view. However, I found I could not voice the settlers. The characters that came to me were Roanoke. I tell you this not as a justification, but to share the process. I really cannot explain it myself, why I was moved to compulsion to write from the point of view of a people who had lived on this shore since the beginning of history, an eastern woodland people of the Algonquian language group

While it is fiction, the action is based on historical facts and is meant to be as true to life back then as is possible from our distance of 500 years. Everything in this book is extensively researched. What people ate, their homes, their beliefs are all taken from existing knowledge, notably the Mashantucket Pequot Museum and Research Center in Foxwoods, Connecticut, and the Wampanoag Village at Plimoth Plantation in Plymouth, Massachusetts. The songs and stories are not Roanoke; those have not survived, but they are Algonquian and I hope representative of what was in the hearts of the people who once thrived. Where I have borrowed, I have credited.

Another hope is that those reading *A Roanoke Story* will come to realize that Americans have absorbed from Native Peoples many values that are not-European: an understanding of the wilderness as something holy, a willingness to adapt to new things and ideas, and a sense of a community as a group of willing participants, delineated by heart and not solely by blood.

The stories in the book are taken from the following sources:

p. 24: From the Algonquin: Kichi-Odgig, the great fisher weasel.

p 46: From the Algonquin: Nanabohzo and Malsum.

p. 97: From the Algonquian: Flood story.

pp. 150, 173: From the Algonquian: An Algonquian Poem.

p. 168: From the Anishinabe: Mi-she-kae, a story of the first people.

Acknowledgments

This book has had multiple iterations, and many readers along the way. I value each one for their insight and attention. In no particular order, thank you to: Ann Marie Monzione, Merry Glosband, Mia Morgan, Charlotte Leblang, Donna Ceglia, Kitty Babakian, Amy Forman, and Sami Lawlor.

My deep thanks to a team of people whose support is bottomless: my fearless writing group: Margaret Eckman, Lana Owens, and Laura Smith. Heartfelt thanks as well go to my publisher Dean Papademetriou, for his support and meticulous attention.

Thank you to Dale Sauter, Head of Manuscripts and Rare Books at the Joyner Library, University of North Carolina Greenville, who kindly left me alone in a quiet room with a pair of white gloves and Harriot's account of the Roanoke, *A Briefe and True Report of the New Found Land of Virginia*, published by DeBrys in the late 1500s; a book of White's water colors done after his return from Roanoke, also published by DeBrys; and artifacts from the site where scholars believe Lane built his fort. After having spent years reading on the subject, to touch and see these items was a great treat.

Last but not least, thank you to Russell, the rock on whom all else is built.

Deahn Berrini

Literary and Poetry Books from Somerset Hall Press

Nicos Alexiou, *Astoria: Exile People Places: Poems.*

Deahn Berrini, *Milkweed: A Novel.* A community copes with a beloved son returning from war.

Lili Bita, *Fleshfire: Love Poems.*

Lili Bita, *Sister of Darkness: A Memoir.* The powerful story of a woman's journey of self-discovery and personal liberation.

Lili Bita, *The Storm Rider: A Memoir.* A story of intense maternal love for her son, and grief for his loss.

Lili Bita and Robert Zaller, trans., *Thirty Years in the Rain: The Selected Poetry of Nikiforos Vrettakos.* Poems by one of the most celebrated twentieth-century Greek poets.

Lili Bita, *The Thrust of the Blade: Poems.*

Lili Bita, *Women of Fire and Blood: Poems.* A feminist reimagining of the women of antiquity.

Tanya Contos, *The Tide Clock and other Poems.*

Roger Finch, *Stations of the Sun.* Poems inspired by life and travels in Asia.

James Hatch, *The Green Behind Every Shape: Poems.*

Penelope Karageorge, *The Neon Suitcase: Poems.*

Dean Kostos, ed., *Pomegranate Seeds: An Anthology of Greek-American Poetry.*

Dean Papademetriou, ed., *Golden Anthology: Writings of a Greek-American Soldier in Korea.* Poems and stories by a Greek immigrant who was killed while heroically serving in the United States Army in Korea.

Shinjo: *Reflections.* Thoughts and sayings of a Buddhist master.

Stelios Ramfos, *Fate and Ambiguity in Oedipus the King*, translated by Norman Russell. A literary and philosophical reflection on the world-famous play, with a Foreword by renowned actor Olympia Dukakis.

Vassiliki Rapti, *Transitorium: Poems.*

Nanos Valaoritis, *Nightfall Hotel: A Surrealist Romeo and Juliet.* Translated by Vassiliki Rapti.

Robert Zaller, *Islands.* Poems inspired by the Greek islands.

For more information about these books,
including how to order them,
please visit www.somersethallpress.com.